A TRIPLE C RANCH
CHRISTMAS WEDDING

BROTHERHOOD PROTECTORS WORLD

DEBRA PARMLEY

Dedication

This book is dedicated to Delilah Devlin, editor extraordinaire, with much love and appreciation.

Acknowledgements

Thank you to my publisher and friend, Elle James, for your wonderful Brotherhood Protectors World which is so much fun to write in and for working so hard under difficult circumstances to make sure my book came out with the others. I love your world and you.

Thank you to my excellent editor Delilah Devlin, for your hard work editing this book during the Thanksgiving holiday and under difficult circumstances, for your keen eye and advice and for your friendship.

Thank you to my husband Mike Parmley for the many plot discussions, for explaining how to move horses, for cooking dinner, for that first beta read, for putting up with me staying up all night to write, and for the many years of support.

Thank you to Charles Welshans, for beta reading, for tips on rodeo life, Marine heroes, and for your friendship.

Thank you to my PA/and sister Kimberly Lear, for my updated website, reader newsletter, reviewer newsletter, and all numerous things you do, and for being my biggest reader fan from day one.

Thank you to my reviewers and bloggers, for each and every review you leave for one of my books. It is your feedback that lets me know what to write more of. You wanted more and I listen. This is my fifth book in Elle James Brotherhood Protectors World. I appreciate the time it takes for you to write a review. Your reviews help more than you know.

To my readers, thank you for purchasing and reading my books. If this is the first time to read one of my books, thank you for taking a chance on mine when there are so many to choose from.

Infinite love and gratitude to you all.

BROTHERHOOD PROTECTORS

ORIGINAL SERIES BY ELLE JAMES

Brotherhood Protectors Series

Montana SEAL (#1)

Bride Protector SEAL (#2)

Montana D-Force (#3)

Cowboy D-Force (#4)

Montana Ranger (#5)

Montana Dog Soldier (#6)

Montana SEAL Daddy (#7)

Montana Ranger's Wedding Vow (#8)

Montana SEAL Undercover Daddy (#9)

Cape Cod SEAL Rescue (#10)

Montana SEAL Friendly Fire (#11)

Montana SEAL's Mail-Order Bride (#12)

SEAL Justice (#13)

Ranger Creed (#14)

Delta Force Strong (#15)

Montana Rescue (Sleeper SEAL)

Hot SEAL Salty Dog (SEALs in Paradise)

Hot SEAL Hawaiian Nights (SEALs in Paradise)

CHAPTER 1

Eagle Rock, Montana

"GUNNY, when are you going to ask Lucy Woods to marry you?" Hank "Montana" Patterson, CEO of Brotherhood Protectors asked.

Gunnery sergeant Jack "Gunny" Barr had stopped by the Brotherhood Protectors office to pick up his next assignment. The former Marine enjoyed working for Hank and being a part of the brotherhood, all of whom were veterans.

He thought about the engagement ring currently tucked inside his pocket. The custom-ordered ring had turned out exactly as he'd wanted, after weeks of deliberation over the design.

How do you surprise and please a woman who is a jewelry designer?

You watch her for a month, as she designs and creates jewelry of her own, to learn what she likes, what she dislikes, and you listen to her very closely.

She'd thought he was just interested in her business and being supportive. She'd had no idea he had another motive.

He'd been waiting for the right moment to ask Lucy to marry him but, so far, that moment hadn't arrived. The guys had been teasing him about when he would ask her, but this was the first time Hank had brought it up.

Hank was waiting for an answer, but Jack wasn't sure what to tell him.

"Soon," Jack mumbled, though he had no idea how much longer "soon" would be. Impatience and nervousness—unfamiliar emotions, at least to him —had ridden him ever since he'd picked up the custom designed ring.

Lucy was so busy getting her new jewelry design business off the ground that she had little time left for romance. Her online store, Bedazzled and Bejeweled, was on hold while she filled custom orders for a jewelry store in Bozeman, which catered to customers from all over the world and had started carrying her designs.

Hank held out a folder to Jack with the information he would need to familiarize himself with before his next assignment.

Jack took the folder and flipped the front page open, glancing down at it. "Another actress," he said.

"Yes. Her boyfriend just broke things off, but he's also an actor, so there's nothing unusual there. She has a premiere to attend and several other events. Basic bodyguard service for a month, and then I'll cycle you back here."

One thing they'd all learned about Hollywood actresses was that many of them had fantasies of making it with their bodyguard. Cycling the men with shorter assignments prevented close attachments.

Jack's first job with the Brotherhood Protectors had been protecting the actress, Angelica Glory, from a love obsessed stalker. It turned out he'd also needed to protect her assistant, Lucy Woods, as well. Since then, he'd guarded many celebrities, but none of the jobs since, or in the future would be as memorable as his first job.

He'd fallen in love with Lucy and hoped to make her his wife.

L.A. wasn't Jack's favorite place, but he hadn't asked Hank to exclude him from any out of state assignments yet. If Lucy said "yes," he would. There'd be a wedding and a honeymoon to work around.

"When do you want me there?" he asked.

"Tomorrow or Friday," Hank said. "Depends on how early you want to get there. She has a luncheon on Saturday, which isn't in the folder, because her manager forgot to tell us."

"Great," Jack said. "I'll go Friday. That gives me tonight to ask Lucy."

"Good luck." Hank grinned at him. "She's a great gal."

"Thanks." Jack's thoughts were already on tonight, and how he would ask her—not on the upcoming job. Warmth spread through his chest at the thought of seeing her again.

The image of Lucy in his mind led his thoughts away. The way her big blue eyes lit up when she saw him always made his day. Her long, black hair was soft, touchable and shone in the right lighting. Her pink, kissable lips tasted so good when they kissed. To Jack, she was the most beautiful woman in the world, and the most loving woman he had ever known.

Lucy was more than just a 'great gal.' She was the love of his life, and whether she said yes, or no tonight, she would always be the woman who held his heart.

Realizing his mind had drifted, he redirected his thoughts.

He would pop the question, get her answer, and then refocus on what he needed to do for the job.

"Anything else I need to know about this job?" he asked.

"Nope," Hank said. "You've got everything."

"Good," Jack said.

He didn't realize his knee had been bouncing up and down, until Hank looked pointedly at it and said, "The sooner you ask her, the sooner you'll get over that case of nerves."

Jack forced his knee to be still and raised his eyebrows. "What nerves? I'm cool."

"Right," Hank said with a knowing smile.

LUCY WISHED HER BOYFRIEND, JACK "GUNNY" Barr, wasn't leaving again so soon. She never called him

"Gunny" unless they were with the men of the Brotherhood Protectors, because she much preferred calling him Jack. And he didn't care which name she used.

Tall, with dark hair and brown eyes, which made her feel all warm and gooey inside when he looked at her a certain way, Jack was her dream man in every way.

Who would have guessed when I came to Montana with my boss, to hide from that crazy stalker, that I would meet the love of my life?

She looked up into those eyes and smiled clear down to her bones.

It was always a good evening when Jack was near.

"Let's go for a walk," Jack said. "Gaze at those stars you like so much."

She giggled.

Every time he took her outside at night to gaze at the stars, he ended up kissing her before they were done. "I'd love to," she said.

One of her favorite things in the world was going stargazing with him. But even better was the kissing. She smiled, keeping her thoughts to herself.

Here in Montana, the night sky was clear when the clouds moved past, and you could see all the stars—unlike outside her apartment back in L.A., where smog and light pollution got in the way. That place had been the worst she'd ever lived when it came to seeing the stars.

Since leaving L.A., she'd enjoyed an extended stay in a hotel in Bozeman while working on getting her jewelry business off the ground there. She'd moved to be near Jack, who lived in a small apartment in Bozeman, and she loved Montana, especially the night sky there.

The stars would be especially pretty tonight.

He grabbed both their coats from the chair, helped her into her coat then put his own on, before leading her from his apartment, outside into the cooler September night air.

They walked toward the park and crossed the street. After they entered the park, they headed towards the gazebo, where they went inside the gazebo and sat down.

"It's a great night for stargazing," he said.

"It is," she agreed, looking up at the stars glittering in the dark night sky. "I love our walks in the park."

"I'm glad you're enjoying your time here," he said. "Do you think you'd like to stay in Bozeman longer, after your jewelry business is set up with the local stores?"

He'd slipped the question in quietly, and she was surprised by the new direction their conversation was taking.

Why is he asking? Does he want me to move in with him? Or is he expecting I'll move on soon?

Her stomach started to do butterfly flutters as her nerves kicked in.

They had never discussed any kind of future. It was always about what was happening right now and how much they were enjoying themselves.

We have a good time together, but is that all this is to him? I'd like more, but I don't know what to say. I don't want this to end between us. What if I say the wrong thing and he doesn't want the same thing I do, and then it's all over?

"Well, I really like it here, and I like being near you," she said. "Especially on nights like tonight." She smiled up at him. "I haven't missed L.A., at all."

Though this had come as a surprise to her, it was true.

"And your dream of being a costume designer in Hollywood?" he asked.

Oh. There was that dream she'd had.

She hadn't thought about it since moving out

here and focusing on her jewelry business. Pausing to gather her thoughts, she answered. "I'm enjoying the jewelry design, and things are picking up here. I think, maybe, my future is in jewelry, rather than fashion design. And I'm not sure I can go back to the night club scene with cameras going off in my face. I never really liked that part. It's quieter out here. People are nicer."

"So, you'd be happy not going back...?" he said, as if to confirm what she'd just told him.

"As long as I'm designing jewelry, and it seems to be well received here, yes," she said.

"You're not going to be able to stay at that extended stay hotel forever," he said. "It's going to get expensive. What's your next plan?"

Next plan?

She hadn't made one.

What does he want me to say? What does he want? Does he want me to stay here, or to move on? I don't know what to say to him.

He watched her so intently, she feared he'd see her sudden panic show on her face, so she tried to force her panic down. "I-I really don't know," she said. "I haven't made any future plans yet."

Noncommittal. That was the best answer.

Jack's gaze moved away from her, and he pulled away and stood.

Oh my God. That was the wrong answer to give him. What is he doing?

Her heart was racing, but she felt frozen in place, waiting to see what he would do. Waiting to hear what he would say.

This is it. It's over. His face is so serious. He's going to tell me goodbye.

Instead, he got down on one knee and reached into his pocket.

Lucy gasped and clasped both her hands over her mouth, as her eyes widened.

Is he proposing?

"Lucy Woods," Jack said. "May I have your hand in marriage?"

He is. He's proposing.

The words registered, yet didn't, so she remained speechless, trying to absorb what he was saying to her. Trying to absorb the sight in front of her. His expression was closed, but his eyes glittered in the starlight.

His expression turned wary, as if he was preparing for a letdown, yet he remained there, still down on one knee, waiting for her answer.

She realized she had waited too long to answer

him, and that wasn't fair to him. A rush of warmth flowed through her, and she dropped her hands immediately and reached for his. "Yes!"

He breathed in sharply, taking in her one word, and then let out a breath, just as quick.

Tears of happiness pricked in her eyes, so she had to blink hard to see him. "Oh, yes, Jack, yes, I will marry you!"

He took her left hand and slipped the engagement ring onto her finger, so smoothly, it felt as if it belonged there. And it fit perfectly.

She stood, looking down at her finger. He pushed to his feet to stand in front of her as she held out her hand. The ring was beautiful. A diamond sparkled in the center, and on each side was a deep blue sapphire set in white gold.

"It's beautiful, Jack," she breathed the words out. "I love it," she said, looking up at him again, trying not to cry. "And I love you."

"I love you too, sweetheart," he said. He pulled her close for a deep kiss.

She closed her eyes and leaned closer to him as he wrapped his arms around her and kissed her deep and long.

Lucy forgot the chilly Montana air as they

kissed and didn't notice it had grown colder until he pulled away.

He cupped her cool cheeks with his warm hands, and said, "Let's go back inside my apartment and get warm."

"Okay," she said.

He kissed her nose and then her forehead, his lips warm upon her skin, and then taking her by the hand, he led her back to his apartment where they took up kissing again, this time on his couch.

She was so caught up in being with him, she didn't text or call anyone to tell them about their engagement or her new engagement ring. Instead, she focused entirely on Jack, as they talked about their future together.

They both agreed that marrying sooner suited them better than marrying later.

Lucy had always wanted to make her own wedding gown and had designed the dress a long time ago. She was sure she could have the gown done in time for a December wedding. They could be married before the year was over.

Jack was fine with whatever she wanted to do.

"Guys aren't as into all the details of weddings, like women are," he said with a smile and a wink. "As long as you're happy, I'm happy."

"Jack..." She placed her hand on his chest and looked up into his eyes. "I'd love to be married at The Rise and Shine Ranch, where we met—if we can rent it, and if it's not too expensive."

"We can try," he said. "But the ranch closed, and the owner has it up for sale. I'll check on it though."

She gave him a smile. "Thank you."

"I want you to have the wedding of your dreams," he said. "Whatever you want, sweetheart, just tell me and I'll try to make it happen."

Her smile deepened, and he bent and gave her a kiss, which lengthened into another long make out session.

She loved their make out sessions, and she loved the way he kissed her, as much as she loved kissing him. That they would be able to do this for the rest of their lives thrilled her more than she could show him. She could have stayed there all evening kissing him, but she also had questions, especially now that he'd brought up the sale of the ranch.

After they came up for air, she asked the first one. "What happened to Cayenne and Fanny?"

The horses they'd ridden on their first date

were important to her, and she would always remember them fondly.

Cayenne was a sorrel, a big, tall, red horse who had looked intimidating to Lucy at first but who had turned out to be well trained and good natured as Jack handled him.

Freckled Fanny, Lucy's mount, was a smaller Appaloosa with black and white hindquarters and black dots on her fanny. Though Lucy had never been on a horse before, and knew nothing about riding, the sweet and gentle mare had made her first ride easy.

Her first horse ride, their first date, and their first kiss, that trifecta of happiness, had happened at the Rise and Shine Ranch. She would always remember it. And she'd hoped they could be married at the ranch where they had first met and come together creating that trifecta.

"Branch Masters retired and moved to San Francisco to be near his son," Jack said. "But before he moved, he took the horses to auction. Buck Harris at The Triple C Ranch bought them. So, they're still in Eagle Rock, being well taken care of. I saw them last week, when I pulled that night guard shift at the Triple C."

"Oh, I'm so glad they found a good home," she said. "They are wonderful horses."

"They are," he nodded. "I'm glad they found a good home, too."

"Where did Katie Wells go? And Ben?"

"Ben would be a senior in high school now. I'm not sure where. He might have moved away. But Katie is still in Eagle Rock, working at the local diner. I'm not sure if she still goes by Wells since she remarried."

"I bet they're selling her pies at the diner," she said.

"That wouldn't surprise me," Jack said. "We could go to the diner and ask."

"I'd love that," Lucy said. "Especially if we can have some of Katie's chocolate pie."

"If we can't get the Rise and Shine Ranch for our wedding, I could see about getting the Triple C."

"Would they allow us to get married there? I thought you said it was a women's shelter."

"Not a shelter, it's a center the women come to, after they leave the shelter, to learn skills for their new life. Then they graduate and move on."

"But it's a private place, right?"

"It is. Won't hurt to ask them though. The worst they can do is say no." He winked at her, and she realized he went about the world differently than she did.

Instead of holding back, as Lucy sometimes did, worrying about upsetting people, Jack boldly moved ahead.

Which wasn't a bad thing at all.

He was right. There was no harm in asking. Maybe they would say yes.

JACK HAD FLOWN TO L.A., after promising to let Lucy share their news first with everyone. Lucy drove to Eagle Rock to see Sadie Patterson at her and Hank's ranch.

Sadie would be the first to hear their news, and Lucy couldn't wait to tell her. She rang the doorbell.

"Lucy, what a nice surprise," Sadie said as she opened the door.

"I have big news," Lucy said, unable to keep her secret one minute longer, and to keep a huge smile from beaming out.

"And you're about to bust with it," Sadie said, smiling as she waved her inside. "So, what's up?"

"We're getting married," Lucy blurted, a huge grin spreading across her face, her joy unable to be contained, even had she wanted to. "Jack asked me before he flew to L.A."

"Congratulations," Sadie said, giving her a big hug. "I'm happy for you both."

"Thanks," Lucy said, moving back. "So," she tipped her head to peer closely at her friend, "will you be my matron of honor?"

Sadie grinned. "I would love to be your matron of honor, if you're sure you want me."

"Of course, I do," Lucy said. "My cousin is waffling on whether she is coming or not, and my best friend from high school is expecting a baby and due any day and isn't allowed to travel so far, right now. You are the closest friend I have on this side of the country."

The two women had known each other in Hollywood, briefly, and had become friends after Jack had saved Lucy from a stalker obsessed with her. Plus, Sadie showed off her purchases of Lucy's jewelry to anyone who showed the least bit of interest and had been introducing Lucy around Bozeman and Eagle Rock to help Lucy get sales.

In short, she'd been a better friend to Lucy than anyone Lucy had known since high school. Sadie was also the nicest actress Lucy had ever met. Her fame had not gone to her head.

"Well," Sadie said, taking Lucy's hand and giving it a squeeze. "I would be honored to be your matron of honor and will do everything I can to help you with the wedding."

"Thank you," Lucy said. "Wait until you see the sketches of my dress," Lucy tapped the portfolio she'd brought with her. "I've had my wedding dress design in mind for years."

"I'll bet you have," Sadie said. "And I'm sure it's gorgeous. I can't wait to see it."

Everyone knew Lucy had wanted to be a costume designer in Hollywood and had been designing jewelry for her online Etsy store and trying to get her business off the ground. Thanks to introductions by Sadie, who knew all the local shopkeepers, Lucy now sold her creations in several stores in the area and online.

Lucy started opening her portfolio and pulling the designs out.

Sadie stood. "Let me make us some tea and cookies while you get those out, and then we can settle in and start planning."

"You're baking cookies?" That was the scent in

the air, which Lucy hadn't really noticed, until now. They smelled delicious.

Lucy realized she'd showed up without notice and may have interrupted her friend in the middle of something. It was so unlike her to pop in on anyone, and she wished now that she hadn't been so intent on surprising her friend with her good news.

"Oh, there's just one more tray to put in, and then they're done," Sadie moved toward the kitchen. "And I'm glad you surprised me. This is going to be a great day."

That went a long way toward making Lucy feel better about popping in, but she told herself she wasn't ever going to do that again. It could have been a bad time to come by, and she didn't want to be like her old boss, Angelica, thinking only of herself.

She texted Jack while she waited on Sadie to come back with the cookies and tea.

Sadie said yes to being my maid of honor. Now, we are wedding planning.

He answered. *That's great. Text me when you get home.*

She smiled as she looked at the phone and was tempted to say, 'yes sir,' to her new Marine veteran fiancé. Instead, she texted a happy face and an, *Okay.*

He always liked to know she got home safe, so this had become a new habit with them. It wasn't that he had to know where she was twenty-four seven, like some guys who were insecure and controlling, he just wanted to know she'd arrived home safe and wasn't broken down on the highway or on a deserted road.

There were long stretches of quiet roads in Montana and spots where cell phones didn't work so well.

She placed her phone on the coffee table with her To Do list back up so she would see it and waited for Sadie.

When Sadie came back with the tea and cookies and placed them on the coffee table, Lucy said. "I really should have called you first."

"Stop that," Sadie said, with a wave. "This is a very special day. You had a lovely surprise, and I'm glad you're here. Now, have a cookie and tell me more about the wedding!"

"Thank you." Lucy took a cookie and placed it beside her teacup. "The wedding is going to be at the Triple C Ranch. I thought about inviting some of the Hollywood people," she said, "but I really want us to be married at The Triple C, and we can't shine a light on them."

"The wedding should be about you and Jack, not about the guests," Sadie agreed.

"They have rules we have to follow," Lucy continued. "If we have the wedding there, all the guests have to go through a background check before I can even invite them. I can't put the address on the invitations and can only tell them exactly where it is, after they say they are coming out here. They have to sign nondisclosure statement saying they won't give away the location or take any pictures."

"No pictures allowed at all?" Sadie asked, her eyebrows rising.

"Only the official wedding photographer can take them," Lucy said. "One of the best photographers in L.A. is offering to shoot the wedding photos as a wedding gift, but I'm going to turn her down and go with the one the center recommended because we don't know that the L.A. photographer won't leak the photos. There was an accusation once that she had leaked a photo of a wedding that was on a secluded island. And you know how it is with Hollywood people."

"Yes, I do," Sadie agreed. "I think you're making a wise choice."

Lucy smiled at Sadie, glad her friend approved. "So," she continued on, "We are just inviting family and close friends, keeping everything small." Lucy wrinkled her nose. "Honestly, no one from L.A. has even tried to keep in touch with me since I moved out here. Not a one."

"It happens," Sadie said, shrugging. "It's a different lifestyle out there, and most people in Hollywood are caught up in themselves, not really thinking about anyone who isn't in their vicinity. It's nothing against you personally, so don't take it that way."

Sadie, who had been an actress in Hollywood, had experience with moving from the big city to a sprawling ranch in Montana when she'd married Hank Patterson.

Lucy was glad to have Sadie as her friend. She really understood what Lucy was going through and was a true friend, not a 'let's do lunch' kind of friend. "There's so much to plan."

"Then let's get started," Sadie said. "Tell me what you have so far."

Lucy pulled out her cell phone and checked her To Do list. "Okay, so, on my list is a great big tree, decorated for Christmas. Then red and white poinsettias and some pretty Christmas bows and bulbs."

"That sounds lovely," Sadie said.

"I originally wanted to be married at The Rise and Shine Ranch, but it's vacant right now and for sale. The owner is a real grouch and won't consider renting it, even for a day. So, I'm real happy Jack got the Triple C Ranch to say yes, with conditions."

"I'm glad, too," Sadie said. "The Triple C is the newest ranch in the area and a beautiful setting for your wedding. Okay, let's tackle your list, one thing at a time. The tree will be easy. We have plenty of trees out here." Sadie swept her arm in a wide circle and laughed. "Great big Montana trees."

Lucy laughed, too. "True. We do!" Then she stopped laughing. "Of course, we'd have to cut one."

"One of our Brotherhood Protectors, Tim Watson, worked as a lumber jack up in Canada. His nickname is 'Timbers'." Sadie winked at her. "He'd be the perfect guy to cut you a tree. You and Jack could pick out the tree, and then Timbers could cut it down and haul it back. I'm sure he'd be happy to help. Eventually, you'll meet all the members of the team. I'll ask him for you."

"That's perfect," Lucy said. "Thank you!"

"You're welcome."

"Let's make an appointment to pick out dresses," Lucy said. "I'll need to pick one for my cousin, in case she decides to come out after all. So, there's just the two of you. My side of the wedding party is small. Jack has more close friends than I do, but he says we can keep the wedding party small."

"You didn't have time for friends, while Angelica kept you running all over town for her. You had no private time at all."

Lucy shuddered. "She was exhausting and rarely pleased about anything."

"I know," Sadie said. "She's like that on set, too, from what I hear. I don't know how you stayed with her as long as you did."

"I don't either. I was different back then."

Before Jack.

She didn't say it, but she thought it. Jack had made sure to let her know when he'd thought she wasn't being treated right and should stand up for herself with the volatile actress, and he'd done it in quiet ways which had made her feel better about herself, while going unnoticed by Angelica. She supposed that was when she'd first started to fall in love with him.

He was so handsome and masculine and strong, but then so were many of the men in Hollywood. But Jack, he was different than the others.

He noticed things.

And he'd cared about her from the start. From day one, he'd treated her with respect, love, and encouragement. Being around him had made her a stronger woman. A smile curved across her lips as she remembered.

"You're daydreaming about Jack, aren't you?" Sadie asked, her tone sly.

"Yes," Lucy laughed. "I've been doing that more, lately."

"But, of course, you beautiful bride to be," Sadie said. "That's what most brides do."

"It has been so nice, eating where I want to eat for a change," Lucy steered the subject back. "And planning my weekend with the things I want to do. When I worked for Angelica, I had no time to myself, but then suddenly I had all my time back. It's been heady. Like the roof blew off, leaving everything wide open."

"You've done great. Look at all the lovely jewelry pieces you've had time to make and how quickly they're selling. Your business should pick up even more, especially with Christmas coming."

"It has already," Lucy said. "I've had to give everyone a date, after which I can't take commissions, because I need to finish my dress."

"Well, we're going to knock out this wedding planning and delegate who is doing what, so you can get back to finishing your dress. I know that is a labor of love."

"It is," Lucy nodded. "I just wish my mother and grandmothers were still alive to see it."

"Oh, they'll see it," Sadie said. "They may not be physically sitting in a seat to watch your wedding where you can see them, but they'll be there in spirit."

Lucy blinked back a tear.

Sadie switched the subject. "What do you want to do for your bachelorette party? That's on me, so I want to know what you've always dreamed of."

"Oh!" Lucy blinked. "Well, I never really dreamed about that part. Just the dress and a handsome husband who loves me."

"Well, start thinking of what you'd like to do, and I'll set it up."

"Okay. I'll think about it."

They bent their heads together and continued planning.

Before Lucy drove back to Bozeman that evening, they nearly had the entire wedding planned, except for the bachelorette party,

She had no idea what she wanted to do for her party. Partying in a club was not what she wanted to do. But it was the only kind of bachelorette party she'd ever been to. Telling Sadie she'd get back to her on that, Lucy headed toward her car in the driveway.

On the way there, Lucy ran into several of the Brotherhood Protectors. They each congratulated her on their engagement.

Lucy smiled, knowing Jack must have texted Hank because word of their engagement had spread fast.

She was enjoying the moment until the newest guy, Dan "Crash" Barnes, former USAF, jokingly said, "I can't wait 'til Gunny's bachelor party." He nudged Barret Williams. "Marines have the best bachelor parties. Last one I went to, we had to dunk the groom in the pool several times to wake him enough to get him to the wedding on time."

"You know Marines," another man Lucy didn't

know said, and then they all laughed as if they were privy to an inside joke which she was not.

At that moment, Hank came out on the porch and called the guys into his office. They all waved goodbye to her and went inside.

Wild bachelor parties and drunken grooms.

That was not what she needed to hear about before the hour-long drive back to Bozeman.

She frowned as she pulled out of the drive onto the main road.

A drunk groom, who had to be dunked in a swimming pool to make it to his bride's side on their wedding day, would not fit in with her picture of the wedding she'd dreamed of and was planning for.

Jack wouldn't do that, would he?

He was the first Marine she had ever known.

For the first time, doubt crept in, nagging at her, as she drove home through the Montana night.

CHAPTER 2

LUCY FINISHED the wedding dress just as December arrived. She was pleased with how it had turned out and got more excited about the wedding every time she looked at it. Now she had it in the back of her car, ready to take it to Sadie's near Eagle Rock, closer to the wedding venue. Sadie had space to store it until the wedding day, which was a better option than the crowded closet at Lucy's place.

Hank had been keeping Jack busy for the last two months. He'd taken every assignment he could, because he was putting together cash for their honeymoon and earning extra money for a down payment on a house. Though he'd put his house in Texas up for sale, he didn't have a buyer yet. He'd offered to let Lucy move into his small apartment, but she'd turned him down.

She was old fashioned and didn't want to move in with him until they were married, plus she also needed extra room to create her jewelry.

Though she'd offered to chip in on the honeymoon, Jack had said no. He wanted to cover their trip himself, and her extended stay hotel was costing her enough. Besides, he kept saying, he made plenty doing the extra bodyguard stuff. He was feathering their nest so he could spend more time with her after they were married.

"Mark out two whole weeks on your calendar," he said. "We're going on our honeymoon, which should be the trip of a lifetime."

Where they were going was a surprise, but she would need a passport. It was a good thing she'd gotten one when she'd started working for Angelica, because those took time.

Though Lucy had pestered him to tell her where they were going, Jack hadn't budged. She had everything she wanted for the wedding, and in turn, she let him handle the honeymoon.

He'd given her a list though. Swimsuit, water shoes, sunglasses, and a swimsuit coverup.

She'd taken to pulling the list out, looking at it,

and imagining all the places they might be going, which required a swimsuit and suntan lotion. With these hints, she was pretty sure she would like wherever they were headed.

This long interlude leading up to the wedding was a lesson in trust. Waiting, not knowing, being apart for long stretches of time.

In Montana, it was now snowing. Light snowflakes sprinkled down upon everything outside the Eagle Rock diner, coating all it touched in white lacy patterns as Lucy and Sadie watched.

The falling snow made Lucy giddy with joy. "Looks like we'll be having a white Christmas. That would be perfect," she said. "Timbers is cutting our tree, right now."

The one thing Lucy and Jack had time to do, on the two days he'd been back in town, had been to go hiking and pick out a good tree for the great room in the main house at the ranch, where they would be married. It had taken them a lot longer than she'd expected. She'd had no idea perfect Christmas trees were so hard to find, and she had wanted the tree to have a straight trunk and full branches.

Just like their marriage would be, full and straight, and healthy.

She didn't want to start their marriage with a crooked tree or one with bad patches. Maybe that was silly, but it was how she felt.

So, they had gone hiking on both days Jack was home, until she found the perfect tree, and then Jack wrapped that tree trunk with a huge red plastic ribbon and tied a big bow, so Timbers would not miss their tree.

"I'm sure it will be a beautiful tree," Sadie said. "And I love your selection of ribbon for the bows, and the ornaments you picked. You know, if you weren't designing gowns and jewelry, you'd be good at decoration and floral design."

"Thanks, Sadie," Lucy said. "I loved playing dress-up princess in old gowns when I was growing up and was drawn to the dresses and jewelry. I used to say I'd make this dress in lavender satin with white fur around the shoulders and no sleeves. That was during my 'put fur on everything' phase, before someone told me those furs were really animal skins. I'm not sure where I thought they came from. A fairy godmother's magic wand, I guess."

They both laughed.

"Looks like you're getting your wish with this wedding and your handsome groom," Sadie said.

"Oh, I am," Lucy said. "Everything is fairytale perfect, so far, and life isn't usually like that. Not for me."

Emma brought them a slice of apple pie to share and two forks before she topped off their coffee.

"Thanks, Emma," Sadie said.

"You're welcome, Sadie," Emma said. "Anything else I can get you girls?"

"No," they said, and both shook their heads.

Once the waitress had walked away, Lucy leaned forward and lowered her voice. "Cousin Rose sent her measurements a couple weeks ago, but now she's saying the dress may not fit her. That her boobs may be too big."

"Oh, no," Sadie said.

"Rose is well-endowed," Lucy head. "Has the kind of breasts men stare at. Now, she's going to be poured into her dress because she's gained weight. I'm just going to say it. She should've known that could happen and been more careful with what she was eating."

"I agree," Sadie said, wrinkling her nose. "That's why we're sharing this pie."

"Exactly. I'd have loved to have a piece all to myself," Lucy said. "But I need to be able to fit into my wedding gown. So, I'm glad we're sharing."

"Me, too," Sadie said. "Your cousin hasn't been very thoughtful. Waiting until the last minute to say, yes, for sure, she was coming to your wedding and to go ahead with the dress. What was that all about?"

"Her boyfriend. Whether she was going on a trip with him or not." Lucy sighed.

"I see," Sadie said. "So, I guess she isn't going with him."

"Oh, she is. He changed the date of the trip so she could do both."

"That was nice of him."

"Yes. Particularly since it was a work trip," Lucy said.

"Nice of his company then, too."

"Well, he owns the company," Lucy said. "So, he has a lot of control over what he can do and when."

"That's not as easy as you might think," Sadie said. "Look at Hank. He can't change the dates he's hired for. He can only say yes or no to a job."

"I'm still able to control what I'm doing with my business, so far," Lucy said. "That's been great for taking off time to do wedding prep things and for the wedding and honeymoon."

"Did Jack tell you where you're going, yet?"

"No. It's a big secret. Says he'll tell me on our wedding night."

"Wow. That is so romantic."

It wasn't feeling romantic to Lucy. She still had the urge to find out where they were going on the honeymoon. Right now, all she could fantasize about was what they would be doing once they got there.

"Hank is flying us to a larger airport," Lucy said. "Does he know where we're going?"

"Nope." Sadie shook her head. "And I was told, that even if he learned where Jack was taking you, he wasn't telling me—to help Jack keep the secret."

"Oh, wow." Lucy's eyes widened. "I figured you two told each other everything."

"No, not everything. There are still things Hank did when he was on active duty that he can't tell me about, because of the security clearance, and I'm sure there are things about the security jobs he takes on that I don't know. And I get that."

"I get that, too. It's going to be the same with Jack, I guess."

"It will be," Sadie said, nodding. "Just because your Marine can't tell you everything, doesn't mean he's doing or has done anything wrong. This is part of the package you sign up for, when you say 'I do' and marry a man like that.'"

"Yeah," Lucy nodded. "I guess you're right."

"And you won't tell him everything either. I bet you didn't tell him your cousin is liable to be busting out of her dress."

"Oh. No, I didn't tell him that." Lucy laughed.

Sadie shook her head, chuckling. "See? We ladies have our secrets, too. Some secrets are okay. Communication and trust, that is what will make your marriage work."

Lucy nodded. "You have a great marriage. That's the kind I want."

What Sadie said made a lot of sense. She thought about the bachelor party and the fact she was marrying a Marine.

"So, how do you get to the trust part?"

"If you give him trust, and it's rewarded because he is worthy of your trust, then it will grow. It can multiply over the years," Sadie said. "But I've seen it go the other way. If the guy isn't worthy of her trust, then she'll have trouble ever trusting him again. I don't think you have anything to worry about with Jack, though. He's a good man."

Lucy's gaze fell away. "I'm kind of worried

about the bachelor party. I heard Marines get wild. That one had to be dumped into a swimming pool because he was so drunk, in order to make it to the wedding," Lucy said. "Is that true?"

"Well, it did happen, but I can't imagine Jack doing that to you." Sadie put her fork down and called for the check.

Lucy knew Sadie had a few other things to do today, and they needed to transfer the wedding dress from her car to Sadie's, so she didn't pursue the subject. It felt better to not think about the bachelor party, so she could focus on other things. Staying busy helped.

PHOEBE "RED" Adams gazed up at the trees on the snow-covered mountain and said, "I've never picked out a live Christmas tree."

"You're kidding," Timbers said.

"Nope," Red shook her head. "Never had a real tree, or any other kind of decorations growing up, because my dad didn't believe in celebrating Christmas. Or any other holiday, even birthdays. He wouldn't let mom spend any money on special things."

"I think that's one of the saddest stories I have ever heard," Timbers said.

They were on the mountain to cut the tree for the Triple C Ranch, for the wedding. Gunny and Lucy had picked the tree out and tied a big red ribbon to it, so it would be easy for Timbers to find.

He was carrying a saw to cut the tree and pulling a sled with a rope to tie the tree to the sled. Then he would pull the sled down the mountain to where his truck was parked, load the tree into the truck, and then drive it up to the lodge.

"Looks to me like a lot of work," Red said, frowning slightly.

"Yeah," Timbers shrugged, "but it's worth it. Special day, their wedding. That deserves a special tree."

"I'd be happy with a little one," Red said under her breath, "Since I ain't ever had one."

She hadn't said it for his benefit, hadn't meant for him to hear it, but he had anyway. He was really good at hearing things she thought he wouldn't. Like he was tuned into her somehow.

"We can cut you one, too, while we're out here," he said. "So be on the lookout for a tree for you."

She didn't answer, and her eyes were shiny and

bright as she swallowed hard.

Looked like she was going to pick her first Christmas tree this year.

Yippee ki-yay and thank you Timbers!

BACK AT THE Triple C Ranch, Buck and Timbers had finished bringing the tree inside the great room of the main ranch house and setting it up. Now, the Christmas tree stood tall in its stand in the corner of the room across from the big stone fireplace. The tree's scent spread throughout the room, bringing a feeling of Christmas. Everyone who entered the room and saw the tree exclaimed over how beautiful it was.

It seemed Lucy would have her perfect Christmas tree and the perfect wedding she had always dreamed of. Outside, snow drifted down slowly. Not enough to cause anyone problems, but just enough to coat everything in a pretty white.

Buck stood viewing their handiwork and listening to the others talk about the tree, while he ate his second piece of pecan pie that day. Emma's pies and cookies were the reason he'd gained weight working at the ranch. His doctor had been onto him, and he knew he'd have to start losing weight after the first of the year.

He told himself the second piece of pie was okay, since he didn't have ice-cream with it this time, and pecans were good for you and healthy.

Timbers went outside to rearrange the little tree he'd cut for Red, which was sitting in the back of his truck.

Buck watched the couple through the big picture window and grinned.

Red's tree had looked tiny next to the big one for the lodge. But Red was so happy, she couldn't stop grinning.

Buck was glad to see her happy with her young man. She'd been an unhappy, cynical, and sarcastic woman when she'd first come to the ranch, but every morning she'd come out to help Buck work with the horses, and eventually, those hard edges had worn off before she graduated from the program. She'd started dating Timbers around that time, and he was a good influence on her now.

It's good to see her happy and smiling.

As he watched them through the window, he wondered what they were saying. Taking a last bite of the pie, he turned to take his plate and fork into the kitchen.

"I'll set the star on top of the tree, after I drop these off," he said to Emma and Leah White Crane, who had planned the tree trimming as an organized activity with the new women residents. "I've got my ladder inside already. Emma, that pie was one of your best."

"You always say that, Buck," she said, smiling.

"Well, you keep topping yourself Emma. I've never known a cook as good as you. Not in all my years."

"I'm making peanut butter cookies today," she said, giving him a wink. "For after the tree trimming."

"Well, now, I hope you save me some," he said.

She laughed. "Always do."

He sent her a happy smile, and then after dropping his dishes in the sink, went on to get his ladder.

OUTSIDE, Red grinned at Timbers. She couldn't wait to put up the Christmas tree with him. "This is going to be the best Christmas ever."

"Because this is your first live Christmas tree?" Timbers asked.

"Yes, and because you'll be with me to help me

set it up," she said. "And this tree is the perfect size for my tiny apartment."

"You'll need lights and stuff," he said. "Unless you already have them."

"Nope." She shook her head. "I need all the things." Her eyes lit again.

Timbers laughed. "Then we're going shopping for your tree trimmings," he said. "Today, before I take you home."

Their plans were short-lived, as just before Timbers drove out of the parking lot, Emma came out the front door waving her arms and yelling for them to stop.

Timbers rolled down his window.

"It's Buck," she yelled. "I think he's having a heart attack or something!"

"Oh, no!" Red gasped, and her face went pale.

"He's staggering and not answering me," Emma said. "Hurry!"

Red and Timbers were both out of the truck and running toward the steps, all thoughts of shopping for Red's little tree forgotten.

Inside, they hurried over to the old man, who Leah had gotten to sit down on the edge of one of the couches. Buck seemed disoriented.

"Look at me," Timbers said, remembering his

USMC medic training, as he did a visual assessment. "Tell me what your name is. And what day is it?"

"Buck," the old man said, ignoring the second question.

"Raise both your arms up, like this," Timbers said, raising his own arms up, slowly, and level with each other.

Buck went to raise his arms, but his right arm wouldn't go up.

"Possible stroke," Timbers said. "Has anyone called 911?"

"Yes, I did," Cecelia said. "I'll call them back and tell them we need a medical flight. Is there anything else I should tell them?"

"They can land out front of the main house," Timbers said. "Tell them to look for the flares. I'll set those up once they're getting close."

"Thank you," Leah said, concern in her eyes.

"No worries," Timbers said.

"No doctor," Buck mumbled.

"Yes, you have to see a doctor," Leah said.

"Got to feed them horses." Buck got the words out, but they came out mumbled, and as if he'd had to put a lot of effort into them.

"I'll do it," Red said right away, interrupting

everyone else who would have spoken. "I'll take care of them for you, Buck. Don't worry, you trained me good. I know what to do."

His face relaxed with worry taken care of. He seemed to realize he wasn't capable of going out into the snow to the barn to feed ten horses.

"Helicopter is on its way," Cecelia called out. "ETA thirty minutes."

George entered the room from the kitchen, and said, "What's going on? Who needs a helicopter?" Then he saw Buck sitting on the couch and went over to him.

"Buck needs a doctor," Leah said.

George nodded and took hold of Buck's left hand, clasping it between his hands. "You're going to be fine, old friend. Now, we'll take care of those horses, so you go on to the hospital and get checked out."

Buck seemed to accept that was what needed to happen and gave a tired nod. His eyes had grown sleepy.

"Don't let him fall asleep," Timbers said, "And nothing to eat or drink. They'll be here soon. I need to go out and mark the landing area."

"How can I help?" George asked him. "What will you mark it with?"

"Flares," Timbers said.

"I've got a couple flares in my truck," George said.

"So do I," Timbers said.

"Just enough to make a square," George said. "Will that do?"

"It will," Timbers said.

The men went outside to set the flares up, while the others stayed inside to watch over Buck.

The helicopter landed, and the EMT's ran inside to Buck. Soon, they had Buck stabilized on a stretcher and were preparing to take him out to the chopper.

Buck looked for Red just before they took him outside. Making eye contact with her, he said, "One bat hay. They pull it. Out on floor. Won't eat. Step everything. You muck."

"One bat of hay every day," Red translated, knowing he meant a bat of hay, which was a smaller section of a bale of hay. She was glad Buck had taught her how to take care of the horses and that she understood him now. "I understand. Or they'll pull the hay out and won't eat it. Then the hay gets all over the floor and makes a mess, so we would have to muck out the stalls a bunch more." She nodded.

"Buck, stop worrying," George said. "We've got this. You go on now, get up in that whirly bird."

Buck nodded once, closed his eyes as if he were tired, and they carried him out to the helicopter.

They all watched as he was airlifted away, except Cecelia, who was listening intently to everything, as she sat by the phones.

LUCY CALLED the Triple C Ranch just before she fixed a light dinner of tomato soup, to see if the tree had been delivered. Surely it had been, by now, but no one had called her.

She'd thought someone was supposed to call her, but maybe she'd remembered that wrong or they had forgotten.

As long as they had not forgotten to get the tree. She picked up the phone to call, and check on it, and waited for it to ring.

Cecelia, their receptionist, answered. "Three C's Ranch," she said. "How can I help you?"

"Cecelia, this is Lucy Wood."

"Oh, hello, Lucy."

"I'm calling to check on the tree that was

supposed to be delivered today. I haven't heard anything and wanted to make sure it got there."

"Oh, yes," she said. "Sorry about that, Lucy. Yes, the tree has been delivered and is set up already."

"Is it decorated now?"

"Now?" Cecelia repeated.

Lucy remembered the receptionist was blind. "Oh, I'm so sorry. I know you can't see it." She rushed her words out. "I didn't mean to make you uncomfortable. I just, well, can you ask someone if the tree is decorated yet? I need to make sure all the things on the wedding list get done in time."

"Oh, yes," Cecelia said. "No, you aren't making me uncomfortable. We just had a scare."

"A scare?" Alarm went off in Lucy's head.

"Our ranch foreman has been airlifted to the hospital," she said. "He's had a stroke, and they're going to admit him. So, it has shaken us all a bit today, I think. But, yes, the tree got lights put on and a star on top. Then I heard the ladies were decorating it with the decorations you had picked out."

Lucy wasn't quite sure what to say next. But she wasn't going to ask any more about the tree right now, or anything else relating to the wedding. "I'm so sorry to hear that about your foreman. I hope he's going to be okay."

"Yes, thank you," Cecelia said. "Luckily it was a TIA and not worse."

"What's a TIA?" Lucy asked.

"That's short for Transitory Ischemic Stroke," Cecelia said. "Most symptoms of a TIA disappear within an hour, though they may last for up to 24 hours. His lasted more than an hour."

"Oh, that's good then, that it wasn't worse," Lucy said. "I'm sure you're all relieved."

"Yes, we are," Cecelia said. "He scared us all half to death. They're keeping him for a while to watch him and make sure everything is okay, before they let him come home."

"I'm glad to hear it," Lucy said.

Another call beeped in. "Just a minute please," Cecelia said.

She spoke to the caller and then she was back. "Lucy," Cecelia spoke briskly. "Is there anything else I can help you with?"

"Oh, no. I'm fine," Lucy said. "It's all good here. No worries. You have a good evening."

"Thank you," Cecelia said. "You, too."

They both hung up, and Lucy sat staring at the phone. She wanted to check on Jack now. No, she needed to check on Jack. She needed to know that he was fine out in L.A., and there were no more bad surprises happening.

Picking up the phone again, she texted Jack.

Busy? Okay to call you?

He texted back. *Yes.*

She sat looking at his response. Did that mean yes, he was busy, or yes, she could call now? She wasn't sure what to do.

Then he called her, and she picked up the phone.

"Hey, babe," he spoke low. "What's up?"

"I was just wondering how you are," she said.

There was a pause, and then he said. "Why? What's happened?"

"How do you know something happened?"

She swore he had such a sixth sense about her, and what she might be thinking. One day she must find out how he did that.

"Your tone of voice," he said. "What's going on?"

"The foreman at the Triple C had a heart attack today, and was airlifted to the hospital," she said. "Oh, wait, no. It was a stroke. I said the wrong thing."

"That's too bad about Buck. I hope he'll be all right," he said. "So that got you worried, and then you started worrying about me? I love you, too, babe. And I am fine."

She relaxed the way she always did when she was talking to him on the phone. Just hearing his voice had a way of making her exhale any stress she'd been carrying. "I'm glad," she said. "I know it probably seems silly, me checking."

"Not silly. Human. Sweet. Caring. But I wish you'd stop worrying," he said.

There wasn't any point in arguing that she wasn't worried, when they both knew she had been, and that was what had provoked her into calling right now, at this time, instead of waiting. When he went on assignments, she worried about all the bad guys out there who had guns.

"I'm fine. I've got to go though, sweet," he said. "Busy working."

"Okay. Love you," she said.

"Love you, too."

They both hung up, and then she laid back on her couch and closed her eyes. That was all she'd needed. To know he was okay, and he loved her.

Everything was good again. And soon they would be married in the perfect Christmas wedding she had always dreamed of. Life couldn't be better.

CHAPTER 3

ZEB BOYD MOVED SMOOTHLY through the snow, skiing cross country, until he stopped beneath a large tree, far enough away from the Triple C Ranch that no one could see him.

Raising his binoculars, he watched the activity at the ranch for several minutes.

He cursed, his breath forming a puff of air he could see, before the wind whisked that puff away. Gathering a handful of snow, he put it in his mouth to prevent another visible puff of air, which could give him away. He'd learned some things over the years about spying on people and casing a scene before he returned to take what he wanted.

There were delivery vans coming in and extra people moving about. Instead of everything being quiet, like it would have been on the ranch this time of year, it was as busy as if they were having an outdoor summer barbeque.

With their foreman, Buck Harris, in the hospital, everything should have gone according to Zeb's plan.

He'd been waiting for months to enact his revenge on Buck, ever since Buck had outbid him on two horses from the Rise and Shine Ranch at auction.

Zeb had even had buyers lined up early before the auction. Then Buck thwarted his plans, and that had been the final straw.

He thought back to their old rodeo days when he and Buck had still been teenagers in high school.

That know-it-all, into everybody's business son of a bitch. I should have taken all his gear, so he couldn't compete. Should've broken his knee.

It still angered him all these years later.

Buck had caught Zeb stealing his pocketknife before Zeb could slip it into the pocket of his jeans, and they'd fought over the knife. Buck had beat the hell out of him and gotten his knife back. Then, feeling like shit, Zeb had given the worst ride of his life and came in near last, a final blow to his pride.

Everybody had known Buck had beaten him up, too, and they'd known he'd tried to steal the knife. After Buck told everyone, the other cowboys had treated him like a pariah. No one wanted to ride with him after that, to share gas or anything else. Buck had ruined his name in the group, and for that, Zeb would never forgive him.

Zeb's embarrassment had turned into raw anger, which had never left him. Just the mention of Buck's name would stir it all up again.

Though the knife wasn't the first thing Zeb had tried to steal, it was the first time he'd ever been caught.

Too bad Buck hadn't been stomped that time I took his leather bareback riding grip, so he had to ride that bull with a rope. Then he'd have been gone from my life for good.

Tonight, would be payback. Zeb took great satisfaction in that thought, imagining every slight Buck had inflicted on him over the years being remedied in one fell swoop.

There was nothing as sweet as revenge combined with a big wad of cash.

His plan was perfect. Buck had been a thorn in

his side for years. At auctions, in Bucks old rodeo days, and now as foreman at the Triple C.

But especially recently, as the old man had been talking to everyone he knew in the ranching community about his suspicions that Zeb was selling horses across the border to the slaughter-houses in Canada. And it was getting harder and harder for Zeb to buy horses now.

Most Americans were not in favor of selling horses for meat. Even a hint that he might unload horses that way could sour a deal.

But in Canada, dealing in horse meat was not against the law, and Zeb was not that far from Canada. Selling them horses was easy. Once he got them across the border.

How the hell Buck knew what Zeb was doing, Zeb had no idea.

But he knew. And he was talking.

It was time to shut him up.

Zeb had been trying to decide the best way to accomplish that when fate had stepped in and helped him.

The old man had had a stroke. Now, he was in the hospital.

Best thing that had happened in years.

Zeb was finally going to get back at the old

man and make money doing it. Circumstances should have made things easier. The Triple C now had ten horses. The barn was full. Every stall.

This could not have worked out better.

I'll take them all.

The thought gave him great satisfaction.

There's not a damn thing Buck can do about it. I'll have those horses over the border before anyone even knows to look for them. The security at the ranch is a joke.

Right now, there was only one man from that security guard company. He looked to be a younger guy, military haircut, likely fresh out, and he mostly stayed inside the main house.

He would come outside onto the porch to play with a toy helicopter, which probably had one of those fancy cameras. He'd come out, play with his whirly bird toy, then he'd go back inside. That was their security.

Not even one camera outside the barn. Probably none inside. But even if they had a camera inside, with Buck gone, it would be easy to cut the camera off.

Their whirly bird boy never came out before three o'clock, and he was always back inside before it got dark.

Maybe his whirly bird didn't work so well after dark.

Or maybe he was too lazy to come out and take a look around after dark, in the snow and cold.

Once back inside, he didn't bother to come outside again.

Lazy.

Just because he had military training didn't mean he wasn't lazy.

Probably a city boy.

Then there was the caretaker, George, but he was only out during daylight hours. Once he had dinner with his wife Emma, he was inside their little house for the evening and into bed early. Both were early risers and, like many aging couples, their lights were out before younger people even went to bed.

Zeb hadn't seen George lately, so something was keeping the old man busy inside.

Good.

Zeb watched as more delivery trucks pulled up and started unloading boxes.

The Indian woman, Leah, met each of the drivers and directed where to take their deliveries.

Something big must be happening.

He saw a case of champagne and several other

boxes being unloaded from the first truck. A florist truck delivered large red and white floral arrangements. The bakery delivered a multi-tiered cake that had white icing with red poinsettias on it. Then a woman got out of an SUV and reached into the back seat, emerging with a wedding dress.

A Christmas Wedding. How sweet.

Plenty of people about, focusing on other things.

That redheaded woman came out to take care of the horses but never before three o'clock, and she was always gone before dark.

Zeb could slip into the barn unnoticed and wait. He could do it now. He wanted to.

No. Timing was important. Impatience could get a man caught.

He needed help to pull this off. The men were lined up, and the truck and trailer were ready. If they were here right now, he could do it. But they weren't.

Buck won't be returning to his quarters any time soon. It'll be the perfect place to hide. He could hide there right now.

Or he could come back with that truck. *That was the better idea.*

He would wait until nightfall, once they were all asleep, and then make his move.

They would come in on snowshoes, lead the horses down the road to the trailer, load them, and then take off.

Once he had the horses across the border, no one would know where they'd gone.

Zeb would have his revenge and the cash.

It's the perfect plan.

BEFORE DAWN, Zeb was back with his truck, his trailer, and two men, T-Zone, and Snake.

Why the hell young men didn't have regular names anymore, like Sam or Bill, he didn't know. But what he did know was these two were good at a snatch and grab. Horses, trailers, whatever you wanted to grab and sell. And, they had never been caught. Zeb wasn't going to work with any man who let himself get caught.

He watched as Snake jumped out of the truck and opened the gate that let them onto a secluded dirt road. Then Zeb drove his truck off the main road onto the dirt road and back to where it was close to the trees that darkened that part of the pasture.

No one will notice the truck and trailer here.

He parked, turned off his lights, and they all got out.

His excitement was starting to build, and he stepped out of the truck, sprightlier than he had felt in years. "Let's go, boys," he said.

They all quickly strapped on their snowshoes, and then headed for the end of the pasture, just behind the back paddock.

"Be careful. Stay in my path," Zeb whispered. He would follow the same route he'd taken earlier that day from the paddock. His excitement and adrenalin fueled him.

The night air was cool and crisp. The moon gave just enough light, and snowfall was predicted to come within a day.

Perfect weather, perfect night, and everything was running just fine.

Following his earlier ski tracks through the wooded area, Zeb and his hirelings approached the paddock gate.

T-Zone reached the gate in the back paddock first and opened it. Zeb and Snake followed him in, while T-Zone shut the gate behind them.

Then Zeb took point. Moving toward the barn, he said, "Listen for that whirly bird I told you about."

"Yeah, that drone," T-Zone said.

"Nobody should be here, but that don't mean the drone won't be," Zeb said. "And I'm going to check Buck's room and make sure no one is staying in there."

He cracked open the barn door, peered in, and then opened the door further to step inside. The barn was dark and quiet; no one moved about.

So far so good.

He moved toward Buck's quarters and quietly climbed the stairs in case anyone was up there. Reaching Buck's room, he tried the door. Locked.

No one was there.

He moved back down the stairs, saw the lock on the tack room, and then headed back through the barn to get the boys, glancing into the stalls as he passed, knowing the horses were there, but double checking.

All ten horses were there.

Reaching the cracked back door of the barn, he stuck out his head, nodded once, and gestured to the boys to follow him inside.

He pointed to Beau, the sorrel gelding he'd

selected to ride. He opened the horse's stall and reached in for his halter and rope, saying, "I'm taking this one. Pick you out one horse and three saddles from the tack room over there." He gestured over to the tack room. "You'll have to break the lock, quiet like."

"Right," Snake said, moving toward the tool bench. He grabbed a crowbar. Then he and T-Zone went to the tack room.

Zeb took Beau, put a lead on him, then pulled him toward the hitching rail, where he tied the horse as he waited on the other two men who were breaking open the lock on the tack room.

He heard a noise which must've been them breaking the lock, and smiled to himself.

One of the horses huffed.

He ran a hand across the horse, settling it, to be sure it didn't start making noise. Then he went back to hitching them up.

After he hitched up the other two horses, he began to wonder what was keeping the two men. Zeb checked his watch.

Thirty minutes. It doesn't take that long to break a lock and grab saddles. What the hell are they doing? I thought I heard them break that lock?

"What's taking you so long?" he called out,

keeping his voice low. "If them saddles aren't in there, start looking somewhere else for them."

He heard another sound which was definitely them breaking that lock, and then the boys came back out with three saddles and wearing big grins.

What are they grinning about? Kids. Probably smoking pot back there.

"You been gone thirty minutes. Where you been?" Zeb asked.

They both smirked but didn't answer. Then Snake said, "Heard something."

Zeb glanced past them, but no one else was in the barn. He shook his head. "Come on now, saddle this one for me. Then saddle yours. We're taking them all. Let's get them saddled up. I want to be on the road as soon as possible."

"Sure boss," Snake said.

He seemed mighty pleased about something.

But Zeb was in a good mood tonight, too, so he brushed off asking Snake about it.

"This one's due soon," T-Zone said, leading a mare to the hitching post. "We ought to get paid for eleven, not just the ten."

"I'll give you a bonus, depending on how much they bring," Zeb said.

This job pleased him so much, he didn't mind

giving the boys a bonus. But he wasn't about to mention that a second mare was pregnant. If they didn't point it out, their bonus would be smaller and that meant more money for him.

T-Zone and Snake shared a glance, as if they were having a private conversation. They'd likely talked about that very subject. Though Zeb didn't care for that much, he understood it.

Making money was what this was about to them. The whole point of robbing this ranch. These boys were much like him.

"Come on now, boys, let's get a move on," he said. "No one gets paid 'til I do."

From there on out, everything went smoothly. They saddled up then tied all the horses end to end. Zeb hooked to four of the horses and the other two men each hooked to three.

"Hold just a minute," Buck said.

He moved to the front of the barn and peered out, before opening the barn doors. He walked back, put one finger to his mouth to signal silence, and then mounted his horse.

The other two men mounted and then they rode out quiet, leading their strings of horses, leading them out of the barn, through the paddock, and then through the open gate into the pasture.

"See if you can send a few of them cows on up to the barn," he said to Snake. "Just a few for a distraction."

If anyone came out to the barn and saw the stalls open, a few cows loose would catch their attention first. Though it was unlikely anyone would visit the barn at night, the more time bought to get the horses away from the ranch, the better.

Snake nodded.

He untied his string of horses and gave them to Zeb.

Zeb and T-Zone waited while Snake rode over to the cows.

Snake got them moving toward the barn. Then he came back and picked up his string of horses again.

They continued on. From the pasture, it was an easy, quiet walk to the truck and trailer. Zeb was pleased with how well this job was going and felt higher spirited than he had in years.

There's nothing like a night ride in the snow to make it feel like Christmas. Everything is perfect tonight. Ho, Ho, Ho, and won't Buck be surprised.

. . .

His good mood did not last long, as at the trailer, it was another story.

Zeb dismounted from Beau, unlocked both trailer doors and opened them, and then tried to lead the horse into the long white horse trailer.

Often the first horse wouldn't go into the trailer. Zeb knew this could often happen. It was night, the trailer was dark, and the horse was skittish to enter that dark place.

After a few tries of pulling the sorrel named Cayenne, a big, tall, red horse, forward and back, with Cayenne continuing to refuse to enter the trailer, Zeb said, "We ain't got time for this. Come on, boys. Got to get him up in here. Go get that cattle prod out from behind my seat."

"Sure, boss." Snake went to get it.

The sorrel continued to be stubborn, but Zeb wasn't having any of that. Not tonight. He kept pulling on the horse, impatient to get him into the trailer.

Snake came along behind Cayenne with the cattle prod. He snickered and said, "Incoming," then zapped the horse on its ass with the cattle prod.

Cayenne jumped up into the trailer, and Zeb,

still pulling hard on the rope, had to back up fast and exit the other door.

Then the gelding was inside.

After the first horse was in, the others almost always went in easy, and tonight was no exception. Especially as Snake didn't hesitate to use the cattle prod at the first sign of resistance from any of the horses. Loading them went much quicker.

Putting the last horse into the trailer, the men closed the trailer doors and locked them.

"There's two mares in there, ready to foal soon," T-Zone said. "So, my count is twelve."

Zeb chuckled to himself and would have nodded, as T-Zone reminded him so much of himself at a younger age.

A sharp eye and always looking to get ahead, that was T-Zone.

"That's right," Zeb nodded. "Twelve. You'll get your bonus, just like I said—according to what I get for them. You done a good job tonight, boys, but we ain't on the road yet. Come on."

They all piled back into Zeb's truck, and he pulled the trailer out onto the main road.

Time being of the essence, he didn't bother to have them close and lock any gates or doors on the property. In fact, he wanted them open so the cows would wander and create a distraction. All had gone according to plan and his good mood returned.

He had his faked paperwork in the glove box. Now, all he had to do was drop the boys off then get on down the road. Not the highway. He'd take the usual backroads.

Canada was his final stop, and he'd press on until he got there. The further away from the Triple C, the better.

When he stopped to drop the boys off, he got out of the truck to tie the horses inside the trailer. There'd been too much shifting inside the trailer as he'd driven, and he needed that to stop.

"They're moving around too much," he said. "Help me tie them up before you go."

The boys helped him tie each of the horses so they would shift around less, and then Zeb was ready to be on the road again.

"Good work, boys," he said. "I'll be in touch as soon as I'm headed back through. You can meet me here, and then I'll pay you."

"Hope you get top dollar," T-Zone said.

"Yeah, those two mares ought to be worth more," Snake said.

They would be, as those horses would be

auctioned separately. Zeb nodded. "Yep. Time we all got on the road. Remember to cover yourselves tonight."

What he meant was, be sure to get with someone who could provide them with alibis for where they were tonight. Always a smart thing to do. Girlfriends, wives, or friends. Snake liked to hang at the pool hall with some buddies. T-Zone had a couple girlfriends in different towns.

"Of course," T-Zone said and winked. "Always do."

Tipping his hat, Zeb climbed into his truck, feeling less like an older man and more like the younger ones, tonight. Once he was on the road, he turned on his favorite radio station and listened to some older country tunes that took him back to those younger days. Soon, he was humming along and drinking a cola to stay awake.

CHAPTER 4

EARLY IN THE MORNING, Jack picked up Lucy, and they grabbed breakfast to go before heading to the Triple C Ranch to see that everything was ready for the rehearsal the next night.

Once she was in the car, Lucy pulled up her To Do list on her iPad and ran through it again, reading off all the items they'd already accomplished and going over what still needed to be done.

Jack patiently listened with the radio turned down low and showed no sign of being bored listening to her.

One of the things Lucy liked best about Jack was the way he really listened. He never made her feel like he would rather be doing something else.

She refocused on her list and read it to herself again, the same way she might have checked to be sure a door she had locked was really locked, or the stove she'd turned off was really turned off. This was not typical behavior for her, so when she caught herself doing that, she chalked it up to nerves. The wedding was getting closer.

The tree should be decorated. The poinsettias should have been delivered. White chairs they'd rented were supposed to be set up in the great room, along with stands for the flower arrangements.

Though Lucy had things checked off her list, she still needed to see things for herself. She wanted to be sure everything was in place.

Jack was supposed to pick up his twin, Ted Barr, at the airport this afternoon, after he looked over the decorations with her, and then the rehearsal dinner was tonight.

She had never met Ted but had seen pictures of him, and she wondered what he would be like in person. Her first chance to meet him would be at the rehearsal tonight.

They would have the bachelor party the following night. She didn't know what the guys had planned, since Jack hadn't volunteered that information, so she was going to have to ask him. She'd been putting off discussing the bachelor party with him, avoiding the subject, but it couldn't be avoided much longer. The wedding would be the day after.

Everything was going like clockwork for a traditional, old-fashioned wedding.

Except, it didn't feel like everything would go off like clockwork.

Ever since the weird dream she'd had last night, she'd been even more worried. Jack had been driving through the snow and wasn't going to make it to the wedding, and even worse than that, he was in danger. She'd woken up, startled out of her dream but still holding onto one thought.

Something is going to go wrong.

"What's on your mind, sweetheart?" Jack asked, startling her. "Other than going down the list for the hundredth time, you've been unusually quiet this morning. I can tell something is bothering you."

Lucy finally blurted, "What's planned for your bachelor party?"

"My bachelor party?" Jack said. "Sweetheart, you sound worried. Why are you so worried?"

"I've heard you Marines get pretty wild," she

said, addressing the biggest thing that had her worried. "Lots of drinking and women. One Marine had to be dunked into a swimming pool to wake him up enough to attend his own wedding."

She blurted all this out and watched him for his reaction, waiting for his answer.

"Hey, baby," he glanced at her, love and tenderness in his eyes, "you've got nothing to worry about."

He loved her, she knew that, and seeing it in his eyes helped.

"I won't even show up hungover," he said. "Our wedding day is as important to me as it is to you. Don't you know that? It's the beginning of the rest of our lives together. I have more respect for you and for our future than that guy. And you're not marrying *that guy*. You're marrying *me*."

He had her tearing up again, her emotions showing, and she blinked hard, clearing the tears from her eyes.

Jack pulled up in front of the main house at the Triple C Ranch and parked. Then he turned to her. "How long have you been worrying about this?"

"Oh, I don't know…" She shrugged.

"No, really. How long, baby?"

He didn't appear to be mad at her, which made

it easier to admit how long it had been. "Since the night I told Sadie our good news."

"Damn," he cursed. "And what started it? Let me guess. You heard some talk by some of the guys on the team, right?"

"Well, maybe…" Then she nodded, admitting it. "Dan said Marines always have wild bachelor parties, and that one got so drunk he had to be dunked in a swimming pool several times to sober him up enough to get to his own wedding on time."

"Marines can party hard. We fight hard, party hard, and love hard," he said. "Marines can be jerks, and some are not good guys. But most of us won't treat our women with disrespect. I've had plenty of time to run around and party with the guys. Now, I'm choosing you to marry and start a family, and I will honor and respect you. I'm no frat boy. That never was my style. So, you never have to worry about me pulling a stunt like that other guy. Even on a bad day. Okay?"

"Okay," she said, giving him a smile.

"So, here's what we need to do from now on," he said. "When something has you worried, you tell me. Then we talk it over, figure it out, see if we can fix it. Sound good?"

"Yes, it sounds good," she said. The relief she felt was immense.

"That's how we need to handle things going forward," he said. "I hate that you've been worried about this for so long. You remember when I told you that I'm happy when you're happy?"

She nodded.

"So, when you're not happy, how can I be happy?"

She watched him and thought about what he had just said, not sure what to say now.

They really hadn't been together all that long. Extreme circumstances had thrown them together and quickly created a closeness she'd never had with anyone else. But they still needed to learn how to be together, as a couple, and how best to communicate with each other.

"Communication, baby," he said, as if he'd just read her mind.

Which she knew he couldn't do, though he'd come close on many occasions.

"Promise to talk to me next time," he said. "I promise I won't bite." He paused. "Much. Maybe just a little nibble, because you taste so good."

She grinned. "I promise."

"Now, come here and kiss me," he said, narrowing his eyes.

She laughed. "Bossy man."

But she scooted over, closer to him, and let him wrap his arms around her.

His kiss was soft and gentle, at first, and then with a growl, he nibbled at her lips. "Told you that you taste good," he said, in between nibbles which moved across her jaw and down her neck, giving her goosebumps. His kiss and his touch warmed her up, even though his truck was now turned off, and no heat was coming from it anymore.

When he'd warmed her to the point where her mind was thinking all kinds of naughty things, like where they might find a quiet place right now to get rid of all the bulky clothes that were in their way, he pulled back and looked deep into her eyes. "All better?"

"Mm-hmm," she replied. "All better, except now I want you really bad."

"Baby, we need to go check on all those wedding doodads on your list, so you can relax," he said. "And then, I want to take you home for more of this, because I want you really bad right now, too."

"Okay. Let's hurry," she said.

He laughed and opened his truck door. "Wait for me to come around for you," he said. "It's icy in this parking area."

"Okay," she said, sounding a little breathless.

He seemed to have sent her into that place of fewer words and more kissing and touching, which he was so good at. But the cold air coming in from outside was bringing her back fast.

"You be careful, too," she said.

As he was coming around the truck for her, she could feel her happiness welling up inside again. It was that floaty kind of happiness she should have been feeling for the last two months, but she'd let her worry creep in to steal some of it.

But now it was back, and she could not hold back the glow she felt coming from inside.

When he opened her door and reached to help her down, she smiled at him, feeling that warmth expand.

He placed her on the ground then shook his head. "Oh, baby. Keep looking me like that, and we're never going to make it inside the lodge."

She giggled while her cheeks flushed with heat, then placed her hand in his and said, "Let's hurry inside then and see to the decorations and things."

He took hold of her hand then glanced across the yard as they started walking toward the steps.

Suddenly, he stopped and stood still.

She glanced up at him in confusion. *Why is he stopping?*

"What the hell?" he said under his breath.

Lucy followed his glance to where a calf was wandering in the parking area.

"Do cattle usually wander around out here?" she asked.

"No," he shook his head. "That's because they're supposed to be out in the pasture. Not wandering through the barn." He gestured to the open barn doors.

"Somebody didn't close the barn doors," she said.

"Right," Jack said. "I've got to go secure that calf." As he stepped toward the animal, he said over his shoulder, "Go inside and tell them the cattle have gotten out again."

"Again?" she said. "They get out often?"

"Once in a while," he said, still moving toward the barn. "Then they need help herding them back into the pasture. Go on inside and tell them. I may be a while."

She stepped inside the front door and called

out, "Jack says the cattle are loose again. He's gone to start herding them."

Cecelia picked up the phone. "I'll call George. He's our maintenance man, but he helps our foreman out sometimes. Buck is still in the hospital, recovering from that stroke. He's not going to be around for a little while."

"Oh, that's right," Lucy said. "How is he doing?"

Cecelia held up a hand and spoke into the phone. "George? Oh, Emma. The cows got out again."

Leah White Crane came hurrying down the hall, pulling on her winter coat and gloves. "Hello, Miss Woods. I heard you call out. We appreciate you letting us know."

"You're welcome," Lucy said.

"Buck is going to be okay," Cecelia said after she relating the message for George and hung up the phone.

"They're watching him for a few more days," Leah said. "But they expect him to make a full recovery."

"Oh, good," Lucy said. "I'm glad to hear that."

"Coming?" Leah asked, as she pushed open the front door. "Takes more than a few hands to put the cattle back."

"Sure," Lucy said. She had no more idea how to herd cows than she'd known how to ride a horse before she'd met Jack.

Being from Texas, he knew all those things. And she kind of liked him teaching her. He wasn't impatient, and he never made her feel stupid. He had a real knack for teaching people.

Well, I guess today, I'm learning how to herd cows, she thought, as she headed with Leah to the barn.

"We saw a little calf wandering around the parking lot," she said to Leah, as they walked toward the open barn doors. "I guess because the barn doors were open."

"It happens," Leah said. "And cows will wander. Grass is always greener somewhere for them. For some people, too."

Lucy figured they would have to find all the cows, herd them back into the pasture, and then secure the barn doors so they wouldn't get out again. Hopefully, it wouldn't take long and then she could check on the tree's decorations and the flowers.

Inside the barn, the stall doors were all standing open. The stalls were empty.

Leah stopped short. "Where are the horses?"

she asked, frowning. "Looks like they're all outside."

"I guess they all got out, too," Lucy said. Her eyes searched for and read each wooden plaque, which had been painted with the horse's names.

Cayenne and Freckled Fanny were the two she knew and felt a sentimental attachment for. She read the others' names and thought about how someone had taken the time to paint these nice wooden signs and embellish the letters with designs that were pretty. It showed her that these horses were loved.

Sunshine, Genevieve, Indiana, Blossom, Petra, Duchess, Silent Storm, and Beau were the other names.

All ten horses are gone. Now, we have to round up cows and ten horses? That's a lot of rounding up. The ranch foreman is in the hospital. What will they do without him to take care of all these horses?

Lucy was feeling overwhelmed and had a sudden bad feeling about things going wrong. But she kept it to herself. Her bad feeling about the bachelor party had just come from worry, and likely, that's what this was, too.

George walked into the barn. "Cows out again?" he asked. "Where are the horses? Horses get out, too? Looks like they're all outside. This might take longer than I thought. We might have to call Dan out here to help us."

OUTSIDE THE BARN, Jack saw only cows in the paddock, wandering about, no horses. He started to look for horse tracks.

As he searched, he got a strong gut feeling about this. His gut had never steered him wrong.

When he found their tracks and followed them, the tracks bore out what he'd been thinking. Someone had taken the horses.

Horse thieves. Do they still hang them here in Montana? Montana had a long history of horse thieving.

It looked to Jack like that history was alive and well today.

The tracks indicated that someone had led the horses out, single file, all the way to the open gate and beyond. The gate now stood open, just like the stalls inside the barn.

Whoever had taken them had been in a hurry, not bothering to close the gates or doors.

He headed back to the barn to tell the others.

As he stepped inside the barn, he saw that George had joined Leah and Lucy.

"The horses are gone," Jack said, as he walked back in. "They're not in the paddock. Just cows. Best look around the barn, see if anything else is missing."

George went directly to the tack room and came right back out, moving faster than Lucy would have guessed the older man could move. "Somebody broke into the tack room last night. Three saddles are missing."

"Oh no," Leah said, her eyes widening. "What can we do?"

"Nothing you can do," George said. "Except put the cows back right now."

"I'll help you with the cows," Lucy said quietly. "I'm sorry about the horses."

"Thanks," Leah said and sent her a sad smile. "Two of the horses are ready to foal in just three more weeks."

"Get the cattle out of the paddock. Put them back in the pasture," George said to the women. Then he turned to Jack. "Show me where they took them," he growled, containing his anger, even as it radiated off his wiry body.

"Tracks are back here," Jack said and gestured for George to follow him.

"Take me to where the tracks are. Then I'm calling the sheriff. I'd better check Buck's apartment when we get back, too, to see if they got into it. He's got a land line. I can call the sheriff from up there."

He followed Jack outside to where the horse's tracks were.

They both looked down at the ground.

"Looks like the horses were led out." Jack said. "Single file. Probably on a lead."

The women were trying to move the stubborn cows out of the paddock, into the pasture on the other side.

Jack watched his bride out of the corner of his eye as he talked to George.

Seeing her trying to move a big cow was sort of comical, as she began by waving her arms and shouting, "Shoo, move on, cow."

It even caught George's attention. "Got yourself a city gal, I see." He shook his head. "She's not dressed for this. Don't let her stay out in this cold too long. You can leave her with Leah, but Leah is a hard worker, raised on a reservation, and used to being outdoors in all kinds of weather. She'll outwork and outstay your bride."

"Honey, why don't you go on into the house," Jack called out. "Tell them what's happened and send Dan out here. Get Cecelia to find the number for the sheriff and call them."

LUCY WAVED and went back inside to get warm and to tell the others.

She was too worried about Jack, and about the horses to enjoy all the beautiful red and white flowers and the decorated Christmas tree. But the scent as she came in the door was wonderful. She closed her eyes and breathed in.

It smells like the magic of Christmas.

They needed some Christmas magic right about now. Too many bad things had started to happen. Lucy stood breathing the scent in and wishing that when she opened her eyes everything would be better and there would be nothing to do but enjoy the beautiful decorations and look forward to their wedding day.

Fifteen minutes later, Lucy went outside to the porch and called out to Jack, who was heading her way, "Come inside and get warm. Emma is going to make hot chocolate for everyone."

Jack shook his head and headed to his truck, calling back to her, "Can't. You stay here and enjoy that. I'm going out to the road to take a look."

"Out where?"

"Wherever the tracks are," he called back, and then got into his truck.

"Wait," she yelled.

But she had no time to argue with him or to run and get into his truck, because he was already reversing and backing out of the drive and onto the dirt road.

In minutes, he was out of sight, leaving nothing but tracks in the snow.

The drone guy, Dan, came out onto the porch and stood next to her, holding his drone. "Has he got his phone on him?" he asked.

"Yes, I think so," she said.

"I'll call him when I get my drone in the air."

The drone guy appeared so excited to use his drone that Lucy wondered if he cared at all about the horses or that his teammate Gunny, her Jack, was out there chasing dangerous horse thieves.

Dan worked the drone, excitement lighting his face as it took off and flew. "Finally, something to look at besides snow," he said. "Take my phone and call your boyfriend."

"Fiancé," she corrected him.

"Call Gunny, so I can talk to him," Dan said.

This guy was already getting on her nerves, but she dialed anyway. "Jack," she said, when he answered, "please be careful."

"Gunny, it's Dan," he shouted, interrupting her and taking the phone away from her with one hand as he flew the drone with his other. "I've got my drone in the air."

This is all about him flying his drone.

"I'm starting where you picked up the tracks and will see where they went from there. So, go on out to the road, and I'll direct you from there, once I figure out where they came out to load them. Had to be somewhere near the road," he said, and then he listened for a moment.

Jack was asking him something about tracks in the snow, but she couldn't make it all out.

"Not a problem," Dan said. "My drone can pick up tracks in the snow, easy. I've been practicing with it every day. I'll call you back once I have them. Probably be ten minutes tops."

Lucy went back inside, leaving the men to talk and to look for the tracks. They didn't need her, and she wanted to move away from Dan.

I just don't like that guy, she thought. *Team guy or not.*

Lucy felt sick to her stomach.

The horses are gone. Now, Jack has gone racing off after the horse thieves to play detective, by himself. Tracking them. And our wedding is in two days. Jack's brother is flying in, today. Jack is supposed to pick him up at the airport before the rehearsal. Which is tonight. We're already cutting it close with our timeline—and Jack's bachelor party is tomorrow night.

I was afraid something bad was going to happen before our wedding. Now it has.

CHAPTER 5

JACK PICKED up his cell phone as he drove and called George.

George answered the phone. "Hello?"

"George, this is Jack," he said.

"What did you find?" George asked.

"Dan used his drone to find their tracks. He found the ruts left by the truck and trailer, out near the main road where they pulled over to load them. It's that dirt access road in the pasture, behind the paddock. They came up that way and took them. He can see where they pulled out onto the road, and which direction they went. So, I'm on the road to follow them."

"I've talked to the sheriff, and he's on his way out here," George said.

"Great," Jack said.

"Keep me posted on what you find," George said.

"Will do," Jack said.

"I'm calling Buck next. The sheriff wants a list of what we know is missing and any information you can give us," George said. "They busted into Buck's apartment and the cases are empty where he kept his prize-winning rodeo buckles."

"Damn," Jack said. "Sounds personal. It would be hard to fence such distinctive items."

"I agree it does. Buck's real proud of those buckles and rightly so. I hate to break this to Buck, while he's in the hospital, after he's just had one stroke."

"We're going to catch them," Jack said. "Maybe you won't have to."

"I'm just going to tell the sheriff I know they are missing along with the horses and hope that the sheriff can call Buck later to get a description," George said. "It's going to be hard enough to tell him the horses are gone."

"It's hard breaking bad news," Jack said.

"Sure is," George said. "At least I can tell him we've got men from the Protectors team on their trail. If you can get a description of the vehicle, the sheriff will get the state boys looking for it. He's going to post about the missing horses."

"Sounds good," Jack said. "Keep me posted as well. I'm in touch with Hank. He's organizing our team, and they'll be in the air soon."

"We appreciate all your help," George said. "Hank is a good man."

"He is," Jack agreed.

BUCK HARRIS WAS asleep in his hospital bed in Bozeman when the phone on the table beside the bed rang. He woke and reached for the phone.

"Hello," he said with a scratchy throat, and then cleared his throat.

"Buck, this is George. Sorry to bother you, but I need to talk to you, right away."

Buck sat up in bed, wider awake now. "What's happened, George?"

"Horse thieves, that's what," George said.

"Son of a…" Buck cursed. "How many did they get?"

"All ten," George said. "Barn was emptied, and they took three saddles."

"Dammit." Buck swung his legs over the side of

the hospital bed and stood, looking about the room for his clothes. "I'm on my way."

"We've got people going after them already," George said. "You stay put—you're in the hospital for God's sake. I've talked to the sheriff, and he's on his way out here. He wants a list of what we think was taken."

"We've got to find those horses quick," Buck said. "The brood mares are ready to foal soon."

He wasn't about to waste time arguing with George about whether he should check himself out of the hospital in Bozeman and drive back to the ranch. Then he remembered he didn't have his truck and sat down on the bed again.

He'd have to find another way.

And where were his dang clothes?

"I know they are," George said. "We've been checking on the horses, not just letting Red feed them. But I should have done more. Watched closer."

"No, they were just fine," Buck said. "This isn't your fault. How long ago were they taken?"

"Not sure," George said. "That young couple getting married at the ranch discovered the barn doors open this morning, and saw the cows were out again. They came and told me."

"He let the cows out to slow you down," Buck said.

"You know who stole them?" George's voice showed his surprise.

A sick knot settled in the pit of his stomach. "I know for a fact who did this," Buck said. "Zeb Boyd has been taking horses to the slaughterhouses across the border in Canada for a while now. He's a slick one, and he's got a beef with me. I been keeping an eye and an ear out and trying to warn folks."

"Wish we'd been ready for him," George said.

"There's nothing you could have done," Buck said. "He's real slick, that one."

"I've talked to the sheriff, and he's on his way out here," George said. "He wants a list of everything we know of has been stolen."

"The papers on the horses are in the top-drawer filing cabinet in the office," George said. "And the key to it is taped beneath the coffee can."

"That's smart," George said. "That drawer wasn't opened."

"Good. Kept him out of their papers, at least. But he'll have forged ones, anyway," Buck said. "He's a liar, a cheat, and a thief. Which way did he take them?"

"Tracks show he pulled off the side of the road out front, then moved up through the pasture," George said. "He opened the fence then herded them down to the road and loaded them in the trailer there. We've figured out that much. And now, we've got a team of Brotherhood Protectors preparing to fly out over the roads, hopefully to follow where's he's gone, catch up to him, and then catch him. Gunny, the one who's getting married here, took off in his truck to follow the tracks as soon as their man with the drone figured out which way he headed."

"A drone?" Buck leaned back against the pillows, tired already from the stress and exertion. He glanced at the clock on the wall and realized the nurse would be in any minute to give him another round of meds and check on him.

He slid back under the covers to hide the fact he'd been up. The doctors weren't ready to release him, and he had no ride, so for now, he was stuck here in the hospital an hour away from the Triple C.

"Which way do you think he would take them?" George asked.

"He won't stay on the main highway," Buck said. "He won't take Interstate 15. He'll take side roads. State Route 87, toward Roundup, Montana." He reached for the remote and turned on his TV, looking for the weather. "Have you seen the weather report tonight?"

"No, I haven't," George said. "Been busy outside, putting them cattle up."

"I just turned it on," Buck said.

"They could take 19 out of Grass Range, which will take them up to 191," George said. "Then from 191, they could cross over the border at Grassland National Park."

"If Brotherhood Protectors men are flying in, they can fly into Havre," Buck said.

"From Havre, they'll still have to decide which way to go to look for him," George said. "There's a few places he could cross into Canada."

"He'll go to the same auction house he usually goes to," Buck said. "Might even have buyers lined up already."

"So, he planned this," George said.

"I'd put my money on it," Buck said. He coughed for a moment and then spoke again. "I know he stopped in Havre that time I trailed him."

"From Havre, it's likely he'll cross at Willow Creek or Wild Horse, but which one?" George said.

"He won't take Sweet Grass," Buck said, thinking hard. "Tell the team to turn for Wild Horse after they reach Havre. Zeb has gone to Wild Horse before with horses."

"What about the others?" George asked. "He didn't steal them all on his own. Not that many horses and there were plenty of footprints."

"I don't know who he's got," Buck said. "But he'll have ditched them before he crosses the border. He's always alone at the auction houses. Never did have many friends he hung around with."

"How's he get the papers?" George asked. "Doesn't he need papers to transport all them horses across into Canada?"

"He's a bad one," Buck said. "And he's got a history of trouble with the law. Any papers he has, I guaranteed you they'll be forged." He turned up the TV. "Hang on for a minute."

George waited while Buck listened to the weather report.

"Got a storm moving in up there," Buck said. "They're calling for six inches of snow tonight. Possibly more. They won't have the Willow Creek Crossing open. Getting too much snow there. Tell the team to go to the Wild Horse. Zeb drives a white Dodge truck and usually pulls a white trailer."

"I hope the Havre city airport stays open long enough for the team to fly into it," George said. "If not, their man on the ground will be all we have."

"I hope it stays open, too," Buck said. "See you soon."

"Hold up, now, old friend," George said. "There's nothing you can do right now to find those horses or to bring them home any faster. You've already been a big help. Stay there by the phone in case we need to call you. I promise to call once I know more."

Buck wasn't about to promise to stay in the hospital any longer than he had to, because he didn't like making promises he couldn't keep. The minute he could see a way home, he was going to grab it.

The horses would be upset, and once they were found, they would need him.

Right now, though, the nurse was coming through the door.

"Well, here's my nurse now," Buck said. "Have to go. Call me later with updates."

"I sure will, Buck, and you get rested up," George said. "We have to let the police do their job, and let these younger men from the Protectors help bring Zeb in. You and I are too old to go chasing after horse thieves, and you need to get well. Emma sends her love and says she'll save you some wedding cake to bring when she visits."

"Sounds good." Buck kept his thoughts about staying put in the hospital to himself. When he checked himself out, he wasn't going to tell anybody.

"Talk to you later," George said.

Buck just grunted, and then hung up the phone. It was hard to do more than grunt with a thermometer in his mouth.

"Flu is going around," the nurse said. "We're checking everyone's temperature today."

Buck nodded. Last thing he needed was to get the flu on top of everything else.

Zeb. That thieving son of a bitch.

As soon as the nurse left, he pulled open the drawer beneath his hospital room tray and eyed the pocketknife his grandfather had given him years ago. The Leatherman had meant a lot to him then and meant even more all these years later. He carried it every day.

Buck thought back to the time he'd caught Zeb trying to steal his knife, and his jaw set.

We're going to catch you this time, Zeb, and send you away for a real long time.

Now, he just needed to figure his way out of this hospital and get back home where they needed him.

LUCY COULDN'T STAND WAITING and wondering anymore, so she called Jack. "Hey," she said, the moment he picked up. "How's it going?"

"Just driving hard, babe," he said. "Nothing new. I was just going to call you."

"Does that mean you're speeding like crazy down the road?" she asked. "Please be careful."

"I will. Got a wedding to go to, and a beautiful bride waiting for me," he said, his voice deepening.

His words and his tone warmed her heart and eased her worry some, but only a fraction of an inch. "Yes, you do," she said. "One who loves you very much and wants you to be safe."

"I promise nothing is going to happen to me. I'm not Rambo to the rescue here. The team is putting a copter in the air, and soon the state boys will know what to look for. We're going to catch them, Lucy. I know we are."

"*You're* going to catch them?"

"I mean the police are going to catch them, with our help."

"It's good to hear you say that," she said. "I worry about you. Please don't be a hero today."

He was quiet on his end.

"I'd rather have you be home, than have you be a hero today," she said. "You're already enough of a hero for me. Let someone else do it this time. Come back, and let's do our wedding things like we planned."

"I'm the only one who can follow these guys right now," he said. "I'm already on the road they took, following them. Sorry to do this to you, honey. I know you wanted me to help you check the flowers and all that stuff, but you know what you want and I'm just going to say yeah those are pretty. You don't need my help to check those things. Right now, I have the best chance of catching these guys, until we get someone else near them, following. There's no one else to do it."

This time it was her turn to be quiet.

"Love you, babe," he finally spoke.

Like that makes everything all better.

She paused before answering. "Love you, too."

Nothing will make everything better. He's deter-mined to chase them.

She didn't know of any way to change his mind. Sure, she wanted them to catch the horse thieves, she just didn't want him to be the one chasing after them, alone.

Stuck with this impossible situation and terri-fied that something bad was going to happen to him, she didn't know what to do or to say. She had noticed he wouldn't promise not to be a hero today.

This is worse than showing up drunk, late to our wedding. This could get him killed. He's all caught up in chasing horse thieves, instead of thinking about the wedding, and he's probably even forgotten about his brother.

"Have you told your brother you're not picking him up at the airport today?" she asked, changing the subject.

"Aw, damn. I forgot about picking Ted up," he said.

"Do you want me to go pick him up?"

"No, you have enough to do today," Jack said. "I'll call Ted and tell him what happened. He can rent a car, which would be best anyhow. He kept saying he could rent one. So, that's probably what he wanted to do. I was the one who kept saying I would pick him up. Just thought it would be nice to spend more time together."

"Okay. And I can do the decorations today," Lucy said. "You just come back safe, and in time for the rehearsal tonight."

JACK'S PHONE BEEPED.

George was calling him back.

"Hey babe, got to go. Another call is coming in."

"Okay. Love you. Bye."

"Ditto."

He switched to George's call. "Hey, George, what have you got?"

"Buck thinks the thief is a man named Zeb," George said.

"Has to be more than one, by the prints in the snow," Jack said.

"Buck says Zeb would take this route, heading to Canada." George then explained the route to Jack.

"Got it," Jack said. "Thanks. I'll get on that road and call Hank right away, then he'll get the helicopter heading that direction."

"Sounds good," George said.

They hung up, and then Jack called Hank and gave him the route Buck had suggested they'd take. Both men agreed it sounded like what the thieves would do.

The thieves were avoiding the highway, likely so they wouldn't have to weigh in or have their paperwork checked. Depending upon how organized they were, this route might be one they'd taken many times before, and maybe they'd/he'd paid off anyone on the route to look the other way.

Jack hoped they could catch the thieves, before they got across the border where it would be harder to stop them.

"Got a helicopter standing by, and the team can be in the air within the hour," Hank said.

"Great," Jack said. "Who all is in this time?"

"Swede, Barrett, Timbers, and me," Hank said.

"Great," Jack said. "Good hunting."

"You, too," Hank said. "Stay in touch."

"This phone is the only thing I've got," Jack said. "That and my handgun," He hadn't brought any special equipment as he'd planned to do nothing but wedding stuff all day. He thought of all the good gear he had at home, where it wouldn't help him a bit.

"Noted," Hank said. "You won't need it. You won't engage, only follow."

"Check," Jack said.

Lucy will be happy about that. No Clint Eastwood shootouts with the bad guys today.

Much as it went against his nature, he couldn't go charging in on this one.

After making the call to Hank, Jack called his brother.

It went straight to voice mail, so he left Ted a message. "Hey, Ted. Your plane hasn't taken off yet, so why am I getting your voice mail already? Dodging girlfriends?" He laughed. "Call me back. Change of plans at the airport. I can't pick you up. Chasing horse thieves at the moment."

That would get a return call.

TED BARR WANTED to talk to his new girlfriend, Marcie Hayes, before his plane took off and then things got busy. His twin brother Jack was picking him up at the airport, and there wouldn't be much quiet time this weekend to be in touch with her. It had been a long time since he'd seen his brother, and it pleased him that Jack had asked him to be best man and his wedding.

He'd considered asking Marcie along, but they had just started dating this month, and that was a bit too soon to start introducing her to family. Plus, she was working, housesitting and dog sitting, and couldn't have left town, anyway.

He rang her number. "Hey, babe," he said when she answered. "Just boarded the plane."

"Have a safe trip and have fun," Marcie said.

"Thanks. I will," he said. "How does dinner at that Italian place you like, when I get back sound?"

"Sounds perfect. I can't wait to see you again," she said. "Talk to you later."

"Ditto," Ted said.

Marcie texted him a happy face and a thumbs up.

He smiled and sent her a happy face, and then he leaned back in his seat, turned his phone to airplane mode and waited for the plane to take off.

Dozing most of the way, he only woke when the captain's voice came over the speaker. Soon, the plane was rolling to the gate.

Ted turned his phone back on and listened to a message from his brother, while he waited for them to open the doors so the passengers could get off.

Jack had left him a message and told him there was a change of plans.

Well damn.

Jack wouldn't be able to pick him up after all.

Ted didn't mind getting a rental car, but he'd looked forward to some time with his brother before the big wedding. It was so seldom they were able to get together.

He gave Marcie a quick call, but her phone went to voice mail.

"Hey, Marcie, just landed," he said. "We didn't pick a time for dinner. How does six o'clock sound? Text me back, when you can. Or call. I've got to pick up a rental car now and drive there."

He didn't go into all the whys, just wanted to let her know that he'd be driving and not texting. He could always put her on speaker phone if the car didn't have a hands-free setup.

Ted disembarked the plane and went to the baggage claim to collect his suitcase, and then headed to the rental car counter.

He would rent a car, choosing from what they had left on the lot, which might be slim pickings. Then he would drive from Bozeman to Eagle

Rock, which appeared to be out in the middle of nowhere. But that was where he had to go for the rehearsal and the rehearsal dinner tonight and where the wedding would be.

The original plan had been for Jack to pick him up, then they'd drive to the Triple C Ranch, where the rehearsal was. Ted could change clothes there and freshen up. Then after the dinner, he would go back to Bozeman to his brother's apartment, where he would crash on the couch. Hopefully, a good sleeping couch.

Much as he would have liked to spend time with his brother, he really preferred having his own rental car, and at this point was contemplating finding a hotel room somewhere nearby.

If there was time.

His brother was up by the Canadian border chasing after horse thieves right now, doing that hero to the rescue thing, again. He'd found his bride that way. So, it wasn't all bad. But it could easily screw up their carefully made wedding plans.

Ted wondered how Lucy was taking all this. He hadn't met her yet, but he'd heard a lot about her. Soon, she'd be his new sister-in-law. That would be different, as they had no sisters or girl cousins their age. He looked forward to getting to know her.

As Jack chased the horse thieves in his truck, a team of Brotherhood Protectors was en route by air, flying into Sunburst, Montana. Their task was to search for, find, and follow the thieves until the state police could stop them and arrest them.

For slaughter, the horse thieves would have to take the horses across the border into Canada. But Calgary, where the big auction house was, was only a ten-hour drive from Three C's Ranch. They all hoped to catch them before they crossed the border because it would be hard to know which auction house the thieves were taking them to.

Zeb heard a helicopter flying overhead, low. He reached for the lever action Winchester he kept in the truck, but then relaxed his hand when the helicopter moved on past.

Must be a wreck of some kind, slowing everything down.

There was supposed to be a snowstorm moving in, just south of the Canadian border, and vehicles were now creeping across at a snail's pace, but visibility was still good.

Had to be a wreck slowing everyone. He still had plenty of time to get across the border before the weather turned ugly, if this slow down didn't keep him here too long.

They might not even know the horses are missing yet. Wish I could see Bucks face when he hears that they're missing.

CHAPTER 6

HANK CALLED JACK. "We think we see them. White Dodge pickup, white trailer, looks full of horses. Give this location to the sheriff." He paused, and then rattled off the location.

"Got it, thanks," Jack said. "I'm less than thirty minutes from there and closing in."

"Great," Hank said. "Bad weather ahead and nowhere to land. We're going to head on back once the situation looks under control. Until then, we've got your back."

"Thanks," Jack said. "I'll call the sheriff now."

Both men hung up, and then Jack called the number George had given him for the sheriff.

"Hello, this is Jack Barr," he said. "I'm following

behind the horse thieves that stole the horses from the Triple C Ranch, and I have their location."

"Go ahead, Jack," the dispatcher said. "Give that location."

He rattled it off, and the dispatcher repeated it back to him.

"That's it," he said.

"Thank you for the information," she said. "Do not engage the subjects. They may be armed and dangerous."

"Yes, ma'am," he said, and he grinned and thought, *I'm more than a little dangerous myself, armed or unarmed. If she only knew.*

ZEB FINALLY PULLED his truck and trailer to the side of the road. The border was so close he could taste it, smell it, and see it in his imagination.

If it weren't for this damn snow...

Four state police cars, lights flashing, came up behind him on the road. He could see the lights in his mirrors, but he wasn't alarmed. They could be coming through for anything. A weather-related accident, icy roads, chasing a criminal, setting up a roadblock.

He was just driving through with his load of animals, and he had his paperwork in the glove box.

The police cars drove up and surrounded him, but he still wasn't alarmed. After all, he had his paperwork in the glove box, and what did police know about horses and their registrations? They'd never guess they were forgeries. These papers he'd had drawn up were really good. His forgery guy had gotten better over the years.

The officer that stepped up to his window with his hand near his gun didn't alarm him either. "Sir, I need to see your license and registration."

"No problem, officer," he said, and handed them over.

"Sir, will you please step out of the vehicle?" The officer's tone was all business.

Zeb frowned.

Now, why would he tell me to do that? My license and registration are legal. They're not forgeries.

He opened the door and stepped out slowly, aware of how nervous the police were.

The police waited while he stepped out.

"Turn around and face the vehicle," the officer said.

"What seems to be the problem?" Zeb asked, as the officer patted him down.

"Routine stop," the cop said.

"Okay," Zeb said. He hadn't been wearing a gun, and his rifle was still in the truck. "Can I go now?"

"We'll need to see your horses and their papers," the policeman said.

"Sure," Zeb said. "I've got 'em in the glove box. Just need to get 'em."

"Go ahead," the officer said.

Zeb moved slow, so he wouldn't make the cop nervous, as he got his papers out.

The first cop watched him closely and a second cop stood on the other side of his truck, watching everything, backing up the first cop.

Jack could see the police cars up ahead, surrounding a white truck and a white trailer.

He pulled his truck to the side of the road, got out, and started walking toward them.

An older man, about Butch's age was standing with a bunch of papers in his hand. A cop was asking him questions while another cop stood nearby.

"Yes, these are mine. I just bought 'em," the man said. "A recent private sale."

That lying horse thief.

Jack stomped forward. "Those horses aren't his. He stole them."

"He's lying," the horse thief said. "My papers prove these horses are mine."

"Then they're forged," Jack said, anger building inside him.

"And you are?" the police officer asked.

"Jack Barr, security for Triple C Ranch, in Eagle Rock, near Bozeman," he said.

"The ranch which reported ten horses missing," the officer said.

"That's right," Jack said. "I've been trailing him. Glad you caught him."

"Mr. Barr, I'd like to see your I.D." the officer said.

"Sure," he reached into his back pocket and pulled out his wallet.

He opened it to his driver's license and his Brotherhood Protectors I.D.

An officer held out his hand, and Jack gave them to him.

His security I.D. also said former USMC next to his name.

"Semper Fi," the officer said. "My dad was in the corps, and then I followed."

"Semper Fi," Jack said.

The horse thief frowned at Jack but wasn't saying anything to anyone.

An officer took his papers and went to his patrol car while everyone waited.

Jack enjoyed watching the man sweat.

He's going down.

When the officer came back without the paperwork and said, "Zebadiah Boyd, you are under arrest," and then slapped cuffs on him, Jack couldn't help but smile.

It gave him great pleasure to see the man taken away in the squad car.

It took a little longer to settle what was going to happen with the horses.

The state police didn't have any place to put ten horses, where they'd be cared for and fed.

After several phone calls and lots of pictures, it was decided that one of the officers would drive the truck with the horses back to the Triple C Ranch, where they could be cared for properly, and then Zeb's truck and trailer would go to the state police impound.

They just had to make sure they had everything they needed to go to trial and that the horses would be okay.

Jack and the horses would be home by that evening. But he wasn't sure they'd be there in time for the rehearsal and the rehearsal dinner.

He called Lucy. "Hey, babe," his voice lowered for her. "We got him. With all ten horses."

"I'm glad you called," Lucy said. "I was so worried something bad was going to happen to you."

"Nothing's gonna happen to me," Jack said. "I'm fine. But I've got to drive all these horses back which might make me late to the rehearsal. I can't leave till the police get done here and say I can go."

Lucy was quiet for a moment and he wondered if she was mad.

"It's good to know you're all coming home safe," she finally said. "And I can tell everyone we're going to be late starting the rehearsal. But Jack …"

"Yes sweetheart?"

"Don't be late to the wedding."

"I will neither be late nor drunk, I promise," he said. "I would not do that to you."

"Okay," she said. "And please be careful in that weather and drive safe."

"I will. Got to go," he said. "Love you."

"Love you too," she said.

BUCK, who had taken a taxi all the way from the hospital in Bozeman, was back at the Triple C Ranch, and after checking on each of the horses, was now seated on the couch at the main house with everyone gathered around him, waiting for him to tell the history of him and Zeb, whose animosity went back to the days when they'd both ridden the rodeo circuit.

Now that the horses were back and settled into their stalls with fresh hay, feed, and water, Buck had called the vet right away to have him come out and check them over.

He was especially concerned about the mares who were expecting foals, even though he could see no signs of them being hurt in any way. He was always nervous when he had a mare ready to deliver, despite his many years working with horses, and he would feel better once the vet had been out to check them.

While he was waiting for the vet, he would pass the time by telling them about Zeb.

"Zeb always wanted to win the cheating way," Buck said. "From the first day I met him, I knew he was no good. And he didn't like me no better."

"So, you've known him since you were kids?" Leah asked.

"All the way back to high school, when we were on the high school rodeo team. And then, after high school, when I started going after the serious money in rodeo and set my sights on them shiny buckles."

Leah nodded, and they all waited for him to continue.

"First, he was all friendly like. Hinted that he liked a good side bet as much as he liked to win, but I reckon that was a lie. Zeb wanted to win and hated to lose. And I think he liked cheating as much as he liked winning, because he'd have put one over on everyone. It was his way of proving he was better than everyone else. He's been stealing ever since I've known him."

The sheriff, who had joined them, nodded.

"But that was before I learned what he was doing to the horses." Buck looked around at them all and stopped to direct his focus to the sheriff. "You'll want to know about that."

"Yes," the sheriff said.

"Well, I went up to Canada one time, following a horse that was going to auction up there that I wanted, and to talk to some rodeo guys about a competition I was interested in," Buck said. "I hadn't been riding long, just graduated high school, and had a good job working on a ranch, so I had a little money put back to buy me a good horse. What I saw up there..." He took a deep breath before continuing.

Everyone in the room waited quietly for what he would say next.

"There was this big group of horses being led onto a semi by a guy who wasn't treating them right. He was beating them in the head, things like that. Well, I got mad and asked the people around me, 'What the hell is going on? Why isn't anyone stopping him?' and you know what they said to me?"

"No, what?" Lucy asked, on the edge of her seat about what he might say next.

"They told me 'That's just Irv. He's a kill buyer. One more day, and all those horses will be dead.

He doesn't care what condition they're in, just how much they weigh, for the horse meat.'"

"What did you do?" Red asked.

"I started to go over there to stop him, but a man grabbed my arm and said, 'Stop, son. He can have you arrested. He's got ownership of those horses, and there's not a thing you can do. Even if you could stop that one, another will step up in his place. Canada exports eight million dollars a year in horse meat. There's big money in it, and men who will kill you to stop you from interfering with it.' So, I stopped and had to just watch him leave. I couldn't get arrested in Canada. I had to be back at work the next evening, and it was an all-day drive."

"Oh, my God," Lucy said. "I had no idea. People eat horse meat?"

"In some places in the world, it's considered a delicacy," he nodded. "So, they pay more for it."

"That's horrible," Red said, anger tightening her features.

"Yes, it is. That was the first time I learned that horse slaughter existed," he said. "Like most people in the U.S., I had no idea it even happened. Had never heard of such a thing."

"How awful," Lucy said, her eyes wide with

shock. Many of the women around her wore similar expressions.

"Them sons a bitches, like Zeb, go around buying up horses, and take 'em over the border to sell to the slaughterhouses. I been keeping my eye out for that sort for years now. And I try to let the others know, if someone bidding on a horse has a tendency to take 'em to Canada."

"So, it's illegal here but not up there," Red shook her head. "Well, it ought to be."

"Sellers up there will tell ya, it's the same as selling cattle for meat. They don't see a difference with what our cattlemen do. A cattleman raises his cattle for meat, sells them, and nobody here blinks about it, except the vegetarians and vegans."

"Well, that's different," Red said, getting more wound up. "Not the same at all!"

"Different countries do different things," Timbers said, shrugging. "You'd be surprised at what some people will eat. They're raised to eat certain animals and think nothing of it."

Red frowned at him. "I'm not blaming the children, who don't know any better but adults ought to!" She was fired up now, her face reddening to match her hair. "We raise our horses for pets, or working horses, or racehorses.

We treat them good. Then, these buyers take them up to Canada and sell them for meat? So, they end up in some foreign country on the dinner table? The buyers and those sellers ought to be shot!"

"Many Texans still say horse thieving is a hanging offense," Jack said. "And as many have said, hanging is too good for them."

"Can't hang 'em," Buck said. "That's not lawful. But we can send 'em to jail. And make sure everybody knows 'em for a horse thief."

"I doubt that would matter up in Canada," Red said. "You don't give an animal a name, and teach it to trust you, take your kids for rides on it, and then sell it by the pound for somebody's table. People need to know what's happening to their pets. Or the horse from the racetrack, or the one that's plowed their fields. It ain't right what they're doing up there!"

"Most of the time, if I tell a seller that a man's come to bid on their horses and take them to Canada to sell them, they won't sell their horses to him," Buck said. "You're right that most people don't know. I been doing my best to tell them."

"Good," Red said. "That's important."

"Yep. I been fighting that battle for years. I

knew what Zeb was up to," Buck said. "Just hadn't caught him red-handed at it."

"So, to Zeb, you were the enemy," Jack said. "I'm surprised he wasn't the one who took your prize-winning buckles."

"He's still angry at his accomplices about that," the sheriff said, joining in the conversation, as everyone turned to look at him. "We've got them all on theft," he nodded. "Zeb was in possession of all ten horses. His two accomplices, T-Zone and Snake, were each in possession of stolen buckles. They'd split them between themselves. He didn't know they had taken them."

"They didn't cut him in," Red said. "That's thieves for you."

"So, we knew their claims, that they weren't here at the ranch during the break in, were lies," the sheriff said. "When they were told they'd be arrested for the theft of those buckles, they ratted on Zeb fast, hoping to get a lighter sentence."

"Course they did," Red snorted. "They'd turn in their own mothers, if it got them off lighter."

Lucy remembered what Jack had told her about Red. How she'd gotten away from a crazy ex and his wild motorcycle gang before she came to the Three C's Center for women. Then the motorcycle gang had come after her. Timbers had saved her, and now she was with Timbers, who seemed like the perfect guy for her.

She must know a bit more about criminals than the other women here at the center. She's quite a character. Though cynical, she seems nice though and obviously cares about the horses. I'm glad she's helping Buck with the horses at the Triple C now, while he recovers.

"Not that their confessions got either of them anything extra," the sheriff said. "Neither was smart enough to lawyer up, and now we have them. Not much a lawyer could have done. Our department knows how to dot our I's and cross our T's."

"You do a great job," Hank said. "We appreciate everything you do." He shook hands with the sheriff.

"And I appreciate your help apprehending the horse thieves," the sheriff said.

"Anything else we can help you with?" Hank asked.

"Not at this time," the sheriff said. "I'll be in touch if anything does come up." He tipped his hat to them. "Ladies." Then he turned to Lucy and Jack. "I understand that there's to be a wedding soon. Best wishes to the bride and groom."

"Thank you," Lucy and Jack both said.

"Y'all know how to reach me, if you need anything." Then the sheriff walked out the door to head to his car.

After the sheriff left, Hank said, "Quick team meeting in Leah's room, in five."

The men nodded and began to head that way.

TED, Jack's twin brother, arrived just in time for the rehearsal, which had already been pushed back an hour. Like dominoes, that delay had in turn pushed back the rehearsal dinner.

Lucy realized she kept staring at Ted and made herself stop. She had known he would look like Jack, she had seen enough pictures, but seeing him in person was a bit fascinating to her.

Both men were tall, dark and handsome, but though they were identical twins, they didn't have identical personalities.

Jack had joined the Marines right after high school and had wanted to do search and rescue. Lucy was pretty sure she knew why. The story of how Jack had saved his twin brother from drowning when they were kids had shown he was capable of that at an early age, and she was pretty sure it had deeply affected him.

Ted, on the other hand, had a fear of drowning and had joined the Air Force, because they wouldn't make him swim. She wasn't about to ask him if he ever worried about his plane going down over water.

He'd just bought his first house, and it was in the mountains of the Poconos. Ski country. She'd planned to talk to him about that. She'd never been to the Poconos.

Hmm, she wondered as she watched the two brothers talking together, *Could Jack be taking me to the Poconos for our honeymoon? It is a honeymoon place, and his brother just bought a house there. But, no. Then the swimsuit and suntan lotion didn't make sense. It would be cold and snowy there this time of year.*

Seeing the brothers together was fun, because they truly seemed to enjoy each other's company, and it was clear that they had missed each other.

Ted was a neat and tidy person. An officer and a gentleman. Jack was a little rougher around the edges, because he was a Marine. And while she was sure he'd done some scary and extreme things, he too was a gentleman, and they both treated her right.

Jack and Ted's parents had arrived, as well.

Mr. and Mrs. Barr were staying at the local bed and breakfast in Eagle Rock before flying to Florida the next day after the wedding. From there, they'd be off on vacation, somewhere in the Caribbean on a cruise ship. Since they would have been alone at home on Christmas Day, and would have already seen both their sons at the wedding, they had opted for a seven-day Christmas cruise.

Both sons resembled their dad, with their dark hair, brown eyes, handsome features, and tall frames, although Mr. Barr had gray sprinkled throughout his hair in that salt and pepper look which looked so good on older men.

Their mother was totally gray, but it was a silver color, which went well with her blue eyes. She was a short, medium-sized woman, who dressed conservatively and wore lots of silver jewelry on her fingers and wrists. Of course, everyone was dressed for the rehearsal dinner, so they were likely more dressed up than usual, but Lucy got the feeling that Mrs. Barr was wearing a style she liked and wore often.

Most older women did. Something happened when they reached a certain age, and they cared less about what people thought of what they were wearing. Unless they lived in Hollywood.

The local minister gathered everyone around, and it didn't take long to move through the one practice they would get before the wedding.

Their group was small tonight, and Emma had prepared the meal for them. Lasagna with vegetables for the vegetarians in the group, chicken parmesan for the others, green beans, salad, rolls, and peach cobbler for dessert.

The scents from the kitchen were amazing.

Lucy couldn't believe how good everyone at the Triple C Ranch had been to them, allowing the wedding to be held there in the first place, and then Emma even doing the catering. She'd said she loved to cook for a crowd.

Jack kept reaching for her hand to give it a squeeze throughout the evening. That was code for everything is all right that had been established when a crazy stalker had been after Lucy. It was their way of communicating quietly in a crowd. Had there been any kind of problem, she would have squeezed back and said, "outside" or "inside", letting him know where the problem was.

She was thinking maybe they needed to change the code a little, because she really would have liked to squeeze his hand back. But that would have stopped him in his tracks and put him on hyper surveillance mode, looking for threats.

It will be different being married to a man who works as a bodyguard for a living. Safe, but very different. They think of things most men don't and make plans for doing things most men would never think of, just to have a plan in case things went sideways.

Still, there would never be any man on the planet she would love more than Jack.

CHAPTER 7

WHEN LUCY ARRIVED at Sadie's house for her bachelorette party, she had no clue what they would be doing.

She'd given Sadie no ideas for the party, not even a hint of what she wanted, Sadie had taken it into her own hands and told Lucy it would be a surprise.

Now Lucy didn't know what to expect. She knew her cousin Rose would be here, and Sadie, but as she'd told Sadie, she didn't know many ladies here in Montana.

Sadie had assured her it was going to be great and not to worry about that.

Lucy walked inside, thinking hardly anyone

would be there, but there was Rose, and the wives of the Brotherhood Protectors.

"You realize when you marry a member of the team, you get an instant family," Sadie said. "We're there for each other, whether it be weddings, babies, birthdays, holidays, or just missing our guys. If you ever need something, just reach out to one of us."

Lucy stood blinking tears from her eyes. "Thank you," she said.

"No crying tonight," Sadie said. "Come on. I can't wait till you see what's in the other room."

Lucy dabbed her eyes with a tissue, and then wearing a big smile, let Sadie lead her into the other room, until she stopped short and her jaw dropped at what she saw in front of her.

There were tables with fabric and sequins and beads. There were bras in black, beige and white, in several sizes along with panties, and in the middle of the room, was a handsome man seated on a raised chair, wearing nothing but a speedo.

She started laughing and grinning at the same time, as it bubbled up from her. "What are we doing?" she asked in between giggles.

"Welcome to your Do It Yourself lingerie bachelorette party and, drum roll, ladies…" Sadie said.

All the ladies pounded a drum roll.

"Your own men's lingerie model," Sadie said. "You can dress him up, dress him down, create what you'd like to see your new husband wear to bed, or enjoy the model and sketch him nude, or sketch him in costume designs, whatever you like. You can also make your own bling bra and panties… whatever you like."

"Oh, my goodness!" Lucy laughed. "This is fantastic! How did you ever think of all this?"

"Easy! You love to design, darling," Sadie said. "And you didn't want to go out drinking, or see male strippers, the usual stuff. So, I thought what does Lucy love? Designing! What better party for you than a sexy design party!"

"Oh wow," Lucy said. "I love it!"

"Wonderful!" Sadie said. "Okay you get to decide what you want to do first, design something on our model, or design the bra and panty set you want to surprise Jack with. How shall we start this party?"

"With design something on the model," she said.

All the women cheered.

"For my husband, of course," she said.

"Sure," Rose said. Her well-endowed cousin

came up and elbowed Lucy. "Last night as a single woman. I won't tell if you won't." She winked.

Rose had obviously been into the wine while waiting for Lucy to arrive.

"How long have you been here?" Lucy asked.

"About an hour. I was helping your matron of honor. There's even a bra set my size here."

"I see," Lucy said. "Did you try on the dress, yet?"

"Yeah."

"And?"

"It fits."

That was such a relief to hear. Lucy sighed. "Oh good."

"Wine?" Sadie asked.

"Yes, please," Lucy said.

Sadie poured her a glass.

Acoustic guitar music started to play.

Lucy realized it was live music coming from just outside the room. The musician walked in, still playing, and seated himself in a corner of the room where he continued to play.

"I love all of this," Lucy said, sweeping her hand in a wide arc, around the room. "It is perfect. Just perfect,"

She loved listening to the acoustic guitar. She

settled into a chair, and taking a pen and pencil started to sketch the model, while the ladies started deciding what kind of lingerie they wanted to design for themselves.

Lucy already knew.

Jack was going to be so surprised.

THE NEXT DAY, Jack was bright eyed and not hungover, and everyone was gathered in the great room of the lodge to wait for the wedding to begin.

The furniture had been removed to storage, so there was room for the rented white folding chairs where the guests sat. Any moment now, Lucy would come down the hall where the bedrooms were and would walk down the aisle between the rows of chairs.

A tall Christmas tree stood in the corner between the fireplace and the front wall, each window in the wall holding a wreath and a red bow. The tree had red bows, red and white bulbs all over it, and a white star on the top.

White candles with red and gold ribbons were spread throughout the room, and red and white poinsettias were scattered across the hardwood floor and on the base of the fireplace.

The bridal party wore dark green velvet dresses with hoods, and the men's rented tuxes were of a green fabric which matched the color of the dresses.

Jack hadn't known the men could rent green tuxes until they'd gone to the store to pick out tuxes. Lucy had been thrilled that the men's tuxes went so well with the ladies dresses and Jack had been pleased to contribute to her happiness.

The ladies held bouquets of red and white roses, with dark greenery and ribbons. Even the white wedding cake had red poinsettias with green leaves decorating it.

Everything had been perfectly planned and looked perfect.

So why was he so nervous? Jack waited for his bride and shifted nervously from one foot to the other.

His best man, his twin brother Ted, nudged Jack with his elbow. "Nervous?" he whispered.

"Nah," Jack said and forced himself to stand still.

If a man can stand in formation in the blistering

sun, he sure as hell can stand still for his wedding to the love of his life.

He would force his nervousness away by willpower and positive thoughts.

Soon the wedding march began to play. The old, traditional tune reminded him that Lucy was an old-fashioned sort of woman. Her tastes ran to the traditional, the classic, the elegant.

Even so, when she emerged from the hallway, Jack wanted to pinch himself to make sure he wasn't dreaming and that this vision was real.

She was beautiful. Breathtaking.

Her dress, made with white lace, hugged her upper body, allowing a hint of soft pale skin to peek through, and dipped in front, which enticed him toward her cleavage. Her long dark hair had been curled and fell in waves down her back, and she carried a bouquet of red and white roses with greenery. Her bouquet was filled with red and white roses. But it was the smile on her face and the light in her eyes which were the most beautiful.

As her gaze met his and never wavered, the love shining in her eyes made him swallow hard.

He felt he was the luckiest man in the world.

At the reception afterward, Barrett ran the music using rented DL equipment. The white chairs had been folded and stacked in a spare room to clear room for dancing, and several people were on the dance floor, dancing to a hopping beat. A large group of men were not dancing, however. They were watching Lucy's cousin on the dance floor.

Jack stood watching Rose, with her pink cheeks, pale skin, dark hair, and big blue eyes, also had large breasts which were emphasized by the tightness of her dress and the fact she was dancing hard, enjoying herself. Her dancing made them bounce. He was bemused, and knew most of the men there were fascinated by the sight. It was hard not to look at her breasts, what with them them bouncing like that.

"Your cousin is having a great time," Jack said to Lucy, raising his eyebrows.

"Yeah, she is," she said, smirking as her gaze swept the men ogling her cousin. "I was worried that dress wouldn't fit her."

"Didn't she send you her measurements?"

"She did, but then she gained a lot of weight fast and could barely squeeze into it. In fact, I had to sew her into it before the wedding."

"You're kidding."

"Nope, not kidding."

"Wow. No wonder she looks like she could pop out of it at any time."

"Oh, she is not popping out. I sewed it well last night. But she might have to be cut out of it later."

"Last night? At your bachelorette party?"

"Yes. And it's a good thing we were sewing because I had everything there I needed. I just had a feeling about it and asked if she would try it on so I could see her in it. You can see how well it fits. I'm glad I asked. I really didn't want my cousin flashing everyone at our wedding. That would be…"

"Crazy." He shook his head then laughed. "Well this will be one to tell our kids someday."

"Yes," she said, laughing too. "Someday. How many kids? Two?"

"Two to start with," he said. "More if you want them."

"With you I want them," she said. "Handsome little boys who look like their daddy."

"And pretty little girls, just like their mama," he said. "But in the meantime, we have our honeymoon, and lots of time for just the two of us."

"Oh good, where are we going?" she asked him

again.

"I'll tell you soon," he said. "Before the night is over."

"Oh, you are such a tease," she said.

"Sweetheart," he whispered near her ear, his voice going low. "You have no idea how much I love to tease you."

She shivered in anticipation.

AT THE RECEPTION, Ted sat watching the bride's cousin as he sent Marcie a text.

The wedding was beautiful. Wish you could have seen it. I couldn't take pictures because only the professional photographer is allowed to at this event.

It was a long text for him. Longer than he usually sent. But his girlfriend Marcie had wanted to him to take pictures of the wedding, and since he couldn't, he didn't want her to be disappointed. If she wasn't expecting to see any, she wouldn't be. He was not about to tell her about the cousin with the big boobs. But he grinned watching them.

It was several minutes before he checked his phone again. She still hadn't answered.

It's late. Maybe she went to bed early and is sleeping.

Marcie's lack of response still seemed odd, as it had been hours since he'd sent the first text to her. Even a busy person could squeeze in a few words.

But how busy can she be? She's just housesitting in the Poconos and dog sitting that little cocker spaniel, Ginger.

There was no one around that Marcie knew, other than Ted. She'd never been to the Poconos before taking that job, and had just met him a few weeks ago. Unless she'd just met someone.

Maybe she's made some new friends. A new boyfriend? It just seems weird that she's gone from "I can't wait to see you" to not answering him, at all.

He hoped nothing bad had happened.

Is she sick? Not able to answer her phone?

He hoped not. He hoped she was all right.

INSIDE THE FANCY hotel room Jack had reserved for them in Bozeman for the night before they would fly out, they were finally alone and ready to take off their wedding clothes.

Lucy didn't know why she was feeling a little nervous. She'd been alone with Jack dozens of times before, but this time felt different.

This must just be wedding night nerves.

She had dreamed of tonight, which was now real and no longer a dream.

Could reality match a dream?

The wedding ceremony had. Everything had been beautiful and wonderful.

Now I am Mrs. Jack Barr.

She smiled to herself. Her back was to him and it was time to take her dress off. She needed help getting the tiny buttons undone, but this was part of her design, her plan, her dream. The slow unbuttoning of these buttons and the anticipation.

"Help me off with my dress?" Lucy asked, glancing over her shoulder with a sultry smile.

"Gladly," he said. Coming nearer, he said, "Lift your hair."

She lifted her long dark hair, and he began to unbutton her dress slowly, button by button.

Anticipating what would come next, Lucy closed her eyes, enjoying the feel of his hands at her back, his fingers brushing her as he unbuttoned her dress. She sighed.

"Happy, Mrs. Barr?" he drawled.

She felt his breath on the back of her neck, and it gave her goose bumps. Then he kissed her there, his lips touching her bare skin.

With each touch, each breath, she was warming up, anticipating how they would make love soon on the big king-size bed.

"Yes, I'm very happy" she said. She'd loved hearing him call her "Mrs. Barr."

When the dress was unbuttoned, he helped her as she stepped out, treating the gown with respect. "You made this beautiful dress, and you were a vision in it. When I saw you walking down the aisle, you took my breath away. My beautiful, creative wife," he said.

His words warmed her heart and made her proud of her work and happy with his recognition of it. The dress had been a labor of love. To have him appreciate her efforts made her feel more than she had words to say, and she got choked up with them.

When he held out the dress, she took it from him. "Thank you," she whispered. She hung the dress on a hanger and put it in the closet so it would stay nice. Though she would never wear it again, she wanted to keep it, maybe even pass it down to a daughter or granddaughter one day.

When she turned from the closet, he was there, sliding his hands around her bare waist as she stood in her bra, panties, garter belt, stockings and heels.

"Not only are you beautiful, Mrs. Barr, you are sexy as hell, while managing to look like an angel."

The smile slowly spread across her lips. "Must be all that white lacy stuff."

"But that's not all," he said. "That lacy stuff, by itself, though beautiful, would do nothing for me. It's the woman wearing it." He winked at her.

"Sweet talker," she said. "But I like it, so feel free."

"Shall I help you with this," he said, slipping one finger beneath her bra strap.

"Oh, yes," she said. "Help me with all these things."

He smiled and slipped one strap down off her shoulder and then the other.

Her body was responding to his voice, his words, his touch, and the look in his eyes as he slowly undressed her.

Once the bra straps were off her shoulders, he moved around behind her and unhooked her bra. Letting it drop to the floor, he moved back around to face her. "Now, we're getting there."

She laughed. "Slowly but surely, we are."

He reached out to cup her breasts and bent to

kiss one nipple then the other. Just when she would have reached to touch his neck and his hair, he straightened, and she let her hands drop back down.

"Walk over to the bed," he said. "I'd like to see you in those heels before we take the rest off."

She walked over to the bed then stopped and slowly turned around. Her eyes widened. He had shucked off his jacket and removed his tie already and was now unbuttoning his shirt, all while he watched her. She stood watching him unbutton his shirt, enjoying the view. Soon, it was on the floor, too. The white T-shirt beneath soon followed.

Now, he stood bare chested as she took in the view. "Come here, husband," she said. He wasn't the only one who could give commands.

He walked toward her, slow step by slow step, almost as if he were a big cat, prowling toward his target. The bulge beneath his slacks showed he was ready for her. Quite ready. And she could not wait.

She edged back on the bed, sitting and scooting backward as he came closer.

"Running, dear?" he said.

"Only if you want me to," she said. "I'd fully expect you to catch me."

"Only if you wanted me to," he said, repeating

her words and sending her a wink.

That was the one main rule they had for all their love making. There could be no gray area as to what they wanted, and there would be full communication. That he insisted on good communication gave her a security she could rely on and trust.

"You look so good on that bed," he told her then he reached for her right foot. "Let's lose the heels but leave your stockings on."

"Okay," she said, and smiled happily. She liked the way the new silk stockings felt on her feet and legs. Soft, silky, and sexy.

She also liked the way his warm hand held her ankle, while his other hand undid the strap and eased her shoe off.

With his thumb, he started at the base of her foot, on the heel, and rubbed up toward the ball of her foot. She closed her eyes and moaned.

He chuckled.

"You keep doing that, and I'm likely to have an orgasm before you ever get my panties off. That feels so good."

"Luckily, you can have as many orgasms as you want," he said. "So, don't hold back on my account. That's my job."

She opened her eyes again, looking at him from beneath heavy lids. Arousal built inside her. "Don't hold back tonight," she said. "I want everything to be good for you, too."

"It will be," he said. "Making you feel good is part of my pleasure."

He continued to the other foot and repeated the actions.

She closed her eyes again, moaning when he rubbed her arch, unable to help herself. After being on those heels during the wedding and reception, and then dancing in them, they were tired, and these foot rubs were a little bit of heaven.

When he was done, he moved up to kiss her.

"Hey, Jack," she said, as he hovered over her, ready to lean in for a kiss.

"Yes, love?" he said, smiling.

"You promised to tell me what the honeymoon surprise is. Where we are going tomorrow? You said you'd tell me after the wedding and on our wedding night."

"That I did," he said.

"So, can you tell me now?" She felt how hard he was as he'd lowered himself, ever closer to kissing her mouth.

He moved slightly, rubbing against her, and she

wanted to move, too, against him, but she held still, waiting.

"Yes," he said slowly, "I can tell you now."

"Please," she said. "Tell me."

"Baby, I can't resist you when you ask, looking at me like that." He smiled. "We are flying to Tahiti, where we'll be staying in one of those over-the-water huts."

"Oh," she gasped her eyes widening. "Tahiti!"

In all her imagining, she had not once thought of Tahiti.

Tahiti. That would be like going to paradise. What a perfect honeymoon.

"Yes," he said. "Do you like my surprise?"

"I do," she said. "I do, I do I do!"

He laughed. "I'm so happy you said I do, my love. I intend to keep you naked as much as possible for the week and a half we're there. We can even skinny-dip off the steps on the back of our hut, and then make love again. Does that sound good to you?"

"Oh, yes," she said. "That's why you said I only need a swimsuit or two, a beach towel, and *plenty* of suntan lotion!"

"Right. Because you'll be either swimming or

naked most of the time," he said. "Unless you want to go out to dinner."

"That sounds like heaven," she said.

"Good." He gave her another deep smile and said, "Then shall we continue?"

"Yes," she said, barely getting the word out before his lips descended to kiss her again.

They made love until exhausted, they both slept.

THE NEXT MORNING, Lucy double checked her bags making sure she had everything she needed for ten days away, in Tahiti. She tucked in the surprise lingerie she had made for him and for her.

He wasn't the only one who was full of surprises.

TED STILL HADN'T HEARD from Marcie the next morning, and with the bad feeling he was getting about the situation, he grew more worried by the hour.

He looked up the police department number after finishing his breakfast at the hotel and then called them. He'd slept in after a late night, and then made it to the hotel's free breakfast ten minutes before they closed it down for the day.

Surely, she would be up at this hour. Marcie should have answered him by now. Something is wrong.

He felt it in his gut.

A dispatcher answered.

"Hello, can I get a wellness check?" he asked the dispatcher. "I'm concerned about my friend and neighbor, Marcie Hayes. She hasn't been responding to texts for a couple days now, and that's very unlike her. I'm worried something might be wrong."

"Sure," the dispatcher said. "We can send a car by. Name and location?"

He rattled off the address and her name. "Thanks for checking."

"No problem. We'll call you back, after we check."

Thirty minutes later, the dispatcher at the police department called Ted back. "We stopped at the house, and no one answered the door. Miss Hayes must have been out. There was no car in the drive. But we heard a dog barking."

"That would be Ginger, the cocker spaniel.

Okay, well, thank you for checking on her," Ted said.

"You're welcome," the dispatcher said.

There was nothing else he could do until he got home, except to keep trying Marcie's phone. Now he was anxious to get there and see what was wrong with his girlfriend. He was beginning to be worried about her.

TED AND LUCY flew to LAX from Bozeman and then from LAX to Papeete Tahiti.

After the plane touched down in the small airport, they stepped down the stairs onto the ground and then walked toward the entrance of the airport. The air was different, tropical, as if it had just rained but then the sun had come out to try everything again.

Just outside the entrance, two women holding the small white Tiare flowers of Tahiti awaited them, to welcome them. Using the traditional greeting, placing them behind either the right ear or the left, one woman asked if Jack was taken or available.

He said, "Just married, quite taken," and winked at Lucy.

She giggled in return.

The woman placed a flower behind his left ear.

Asked the same thing Lucy said, "Very taken. Forever," and gave Jack a smile.

A flower was placed behind her left ear.

"What about that woman up ahead who has flowers on both ears?" Lucy asked.

"She is taken and available," one of the women said. Both women laughed. "And if she waves a flower behind her head, it means follow me."

"May I have a second flower?" Lucy asked.

"Oh, you are newly married and already available?" the woman asked with surprise. "Of course, you may." She handed Lucy the flower.

Jack appeared shocked as well.

She took the second flower and then, walking ahead of them all, waved it behind her head, giggling.

Jack is not the only one who knows how to tease.

He caught up with her quick, and slid his arm around her waist.

THE END

BLIND TRUST

Debra Parmley

Debra Parmley

BLIND
TRUST

BROTHERHOOD PROTECTORS

CHAPTER 1

BRIAN MENG KEN AKA "BARBIE," a veteran recon Marine, and the newest member of Brotherhood Protectors, turned to see what his boss, Hank "Montana" Patterson, was watching as they talked about the security at Three C's Ranch.

The Triple C Ranch, affectionately known as the Three C's Ranch, was one of two Three C's facilities in the United States, where women came after they had been attacked or abused. They came to learn new skills in order to move beyond simply surviving to thriving in their future lives.

Not every woman was accepted into the program. First, a doctor had to certify she was clear of alcohol and drugs and fit to travel, swim, ride horses and take self-defense classes. Her finances had to be in order, and there could be no upcoming court appearances. Once at the center, they had to stay until their time was done. If they had to leave for any reason, they couldn't return. Still, there was a waiting list.

While the centers were nonprofit organizations with generous donors, there was a sliding-fee scale based on income. Women were expected to contribute. Breaking a dependent cycle was part of the center's work with victims who'd been attacked or abused, so they were nudged out of the nest like baby birds just as soon as they appeared able to fly independently.

Unfortunately, their "nest" at the Triple C's Ranch in Montana had been attacked and was still under repair.

Hank was watching a shapely, silver-haired woman to Brian's far left, as the pretty woman walked toward a broom—directly toward it, as if she didn't see the broom.

Hank turned away from the conversation he and Brian were having and called out, "Cecelia, stop."

She stopped, turning toward Hank. At that moment, Brian realized Cecelia was blind.

Hank hurried over to her, moved the broom

out of the way, and said, "There was a broom in your direct line."

"Oh. Thank you," she replied, her voice soft, her tone relieved. "My shins have taken a real beating since all these workmen started on the repairs."

"They don't think," Hank said.

"No, they don't," she said. "One left out a ladder after he'd finished for the day, and another left extension cords all over the place. Now, a broom. I'll be glad when their work is done, and things get back to normal around here."

"I bet you will," Hank said. "Where's your cane?"

"At my desk," she said. "I was only heading to the restroom. Usually, there's nothing in my path in this direction."

Brian listened to her voice, the soft tones floating into his ears like a melody he wouldn't soon forget.

She looked too young to have silver hair, but perhaps she'd colored it that way. Straight and silky, it hung to her shoulders. Silver, sleek, and cut straight across the bottom. Touchable hair. The kind he enjoyed running his fingers through.

Brian took in the sight of her, as though she was a long drink of cool water, his slow perusal of her unhampered. She couldn't see the way he drank her in, which meant his gaze could take her in as long as he wanted. He enjoyed the journey.

She wore a pink tank top over full, rounded breasts, her tank top ending just above her belly button as the tank had bunched up. A thick brown leather belt held up faded blue jeans, which molded to her curves.

She is stunning.

"All clear ahead?" Her tone held a note of laughter now, and not an ounce of weakness.

"All clear," Hank replied. "I'll have a word with the workmen about picking up after themselves."

"No need," she replied. "I should've had my cane. The men have been told. They don't listen anyway, and besides," she shrugged, "I need to find my own way around things."

"You're an inspiration to many," Leah White Crane said, as she came down the hall toward them. The Native American woman knew the women at the ranch quite well, as she was the on-site counselor Hank had introduced Brian to before she'd been called away to her office to handle a small crisis, leaving the men standing here talking about the job.

"When women come here with an 'I can't attitude,' and see you running the front office, keeping everything straight," Leah said with a smile in her voice. "It's not long before they lose that 'can't' and begin to think 'I can.'"

"I don't do any more than another woman with my training." Cecelia said.

"Cecelia, I'd like you to meet Brian," Hank said. "He just joined Brotherhood Protectors and will be security on the night shift here at the ranch."

"Cecelia is our receptionist and secretary and lives on site," Leah said.

Brian swallowed. "Nice to meet you, Cecelia."

Cecelia moved toward him, smiling and held out her hand. "Nice to meet you as well, Brian."

"My pleasure." Brian grasped her hand in his larger hand. Her soft skin felt cool against his, as if she'd just washed her hands.

Her nostrils gave a slight flare as she inhaled, and he took in every nuance of her face. He was aware of her scent as well, and their first touch was almost electric.

As he continued to clasp her hand, he liked the way it felt, holding her hand in his. He gave it a gentle squeeze before letting go.

"Likewise," she said, her face looking up toward his with a radiant smile. She couldn't know he was three inches taller than her, though she directed her face toward the sound of his voice.

It's a shame she can't see me.

He was used to how women reacted to meeting him for the first time and the way they responded to his fitness and good looks. Even before they learned he was a Recon Marine. For the first twenty years of his life he had eaten up the attention and the comments, but being a Marine had taught him discipline and maturity and over the last few year the comments had finally grown old.

Cecelia was the first woman he'd met who'd had no reaction to how he looked. It was refreshing not to have a woman fawning over him.

And yet, while they'd held each other's hands, he'd felt something and was pretty sure she'd felt it, too. That chemical reaction of attraction wasn't dependent on sight. Pheromones were scented, drove attraction.

The ranch house they stood inside still bore the odors of the fire which had nearly destroyed the back of the building before the volunteer fire department had arrived to put it out. Workmen were here to rebuild the ranch house, the only building with fire damage, and Brotherhood Protectors were providing security until construction was completed and a good security system installed.

From what Hank had explained to Brian, when he'd hired him for the job, crazy men who'd been after one of the residents had set the Three C's Ranch on fire to smoke the woman out.

Afterward, the management back east had taken the security of the ranch more seriously and no longer assumed a remote location was enough protection for the women. From now on, the ranch would have security guards and cameras.

Brian was one of four men who would work security shifts, rotating days and nights to make sure the residents were protected during the build.

He'd be introduced to all the female residents and staff, so they'd know him and be comfortable with his presence when he roamed the grounds at night.

Outside the main building of the Three C's Ranch lay several charred log timbers from the lodge, which had been removed. Brian had seen them as they drove up to the ranch. Reconstruction of the lodge would be completed by next month.

Brian watched Cecelia walk to her desk and then settle in, fascinated by the way the pretty woman found her way. Once her hand was on the chair it, appeared she knew just where everything was located.

Cecelia went back to her desk and put on her headset again, increasing the volume. The noisy workers were at it again, she could hear them, even with her headset on—every single sound they made, sawing and hammering, and the popping of their nail guns. She'd been getting headaches from all the noises, and it had been making it hard for her to do her job well.

She answered a call and tried to forget about the man she'd just been introduced to, whose voice had made her stomach flutter and whose touch gave her tingles and warmth all at once.

Her hand still felt the remnants of his touch, and she could still smell his scent, which was clean and nicely male. Not every male had a good scent. His made her want to draw closer. He was still much on her mind, even though she was trying hard to focus on her job.

One thing she prided herself on was doing her job well.

"Hold just a minute please," she said, to the

young woman on the line. Placing the call on hold, she reached for the braille keyboard attached to her computer, typed in 'oral surgeons' and did a search for the closest ones in the area, using a program for the blind, which read information from any website on the internet.

The young woman wanted to come to the ranch and go through the program, but she'd just been told she needed to have all four wisdom teeth removed. So, she was worried she'd lose her spot and have to wait again to be let in. With only two centers in the U.S., the wait list could be long, even once a woman jumped through all the hoops to qualify.

It wasn't unusual for one of the women scheduled to come to the ranch to need some kind of medical care, but this was the first one who'd needed oral surgery.

Feeling the braille keyboard, Cecelia saved the information to her list of medical and dental contacts, and then picked up the call again.

"Yes, there are a couple of dental surgeons to choose from. You'll have to go to Bozeman, Montana to have any dental surgery done. One of us would drive you there and back. You wouldn't be alone, and we would make sure one of us was able to look after you while you recovered here."

Cecelia loved this part of her job. Making things better for the women and helping them step into a better future for themselves, one in which they were empowered, gave her great satisfaction.

If asked what she liked about her job, she would have said, putting things together, making plans for the ladies and keeping everything running smoothly. There wasn't anything about her job she didn't love.

BRIAN HAD BEEN WORKING security at the ranch for over a week when he asked Cecelia out. He waited until it was break time and she'd gone into the ranch kitchen for a glass of lemonade and an oatmeal raisin cookie.

She looked up at him as he entered the room. "Would you like a cookie, Brian?" she asked.

Somehow, she always seemed to know when he entered the room, despite the quiet way he moved.

"How do you always know it's me?" he asked.

"Your scent," she said. "It's unique."

"In a good way, I hope," he drawled.

"Oh, yes," she said. "A very good way." She smiled and held the plate of cookies out to him.

"Thanks," he said. "They look delicious."

"Lemonade?"

"I'm not much into lemonade," he said.

"Milk then," she said. "Cookies are always good with milk." She laid her cookie down and moved toward the fridge.

"I can get it," he said. "Go on and enjoy your cookie. You don't need to wait on me."

"Okay." She gave in with no argument and moved back to her own cookie to take another bite.

He went to the fridge, removed the milk, and then found a glass to pour it in.

"Emma makes the best cookies," Cecelia said.

"She does," he agreed. "I could get spoiled, working here."

"I'll bet you don't get many cookies on your jobs," she said.

"This is the first job I've had where I've received even one cookie," he said, with a laugh. "My jobs have been chasing down bad guys, or guarding somebody, or something."

"What, they never handed out cookies? As a

reward?" She laughed. "Someone needs to renegotiate your compensation."

"The bonuses were good. No cookies though." He dunked his cookie into the glass of milk and took a bite.

"Her oatmeal raisin cookies are my favorite," she said.

"They are really good," he said, still munching on a bite.

When they'd finished the cookies, he seized the moment. "This has been fun," he said.

"It has," she agreed.

"Let's do this again," he said. "How about dinner in Bozeman this weekend?"

"You don't want to go out with a blind girl," she said, shaking her head.

"Yes, I do," he said. "But not with just any blind girl. I want to go out with *you*."

She laughed. "I'm nothing special. And anyway, I don't date, I don't do friends with benefits, and I'm done with relationships. But even if I did date, a relationship with me would be a lot of work. Men don't handle that well."

"I'm a Marine," he said. "We're used to a lot of work, overcoming obstacles, and succeeding at our goals."

"Maybe so, but I'm not ready to go out," she said. "I'm safe here, and I know where everything is."

"You'd be safe with me, and I'd make sure you knew where things are," he said.

"You're going to keep trying to convince me, aren't you?" She tilted her head toward him, looking upward, with an exasperated look on her face.

"Yes, ma'am, I am." He nodded, then caught himself, realizing she wouldn't see him nod. "What will it take to get you to say yes?"

"You don't understand." She shook her head. "I'm not going to get my sight back. This is how things will always be. And I don't date. You should just give up now."

"Give up?" He laughed. "You're trying to convince a Marine to give up? Now *that* is funny."

Cecelia paused, thinking. Then she laughed. " I guess it is."

The real reason she wouldn't go out, the one she wasn't about to tell him, was that she was afraid to go out on a date with another man, any man she didn't know well, who might turn violent.

That crazy Elijah Blair, whom she'd gone out with, had turned violent, and back then, she could see.

They'd gone out. But he'd behaved so strangely, she'd turned him down for a second date. Yet even with full sight, she still hadn't seen the attack coming. When he'd come at her with a baseball bat, she'd had no clue.

Now, she was even more vulnerable, completely unable to see an attack coming at her. She would miss those microseconds if a crazy man flipped that switch, and she'd never see it on his face.

No way am I dating anyone. The risk is too great. If I'd been blind when Elijah swung that baseball bat, I'd have been dead. I can't risk dating anyone.

However, she didn't say any of that. She ignored the way his voice reached something deep inside her, and the way his scent made her want to lean in, closer to him. Instead, she just shook her head, picked up her cane, and stretching it out before her, walked away.

Buy Blind Trust Now

ABOUT DEBRA PARMLEY

"Every day we are alive is a beautiful day." – Debra Parmley

Debra Parmley is a multi genre, hybrid romance author born in Columbus, Ohio and raised in Springfield, Ohio. She has lived just outside Memphis, Tennessee since 1997. Debra attended Marywood University in Scranton, Pennsylvania and was the first student to win first place in two categories of the Delta Epsilon Sigma Beta Epsilon Chapter writing competition, in create prose and in informal expository. Her poetry was published in literary journals while attending college. She holds a BA in English Literature.

Debra enjoys spreading love, one story at a time. Fascinated by fairy tales and folktales ever since she was young, she always ends her stories with a happy ever after. Damsels in distress stories favorites, and you'll find this theme in many of her stories. An Air Force veteran's wife, Debra enjoys writing military romance. Veterans hold a special place in her heart.

Debra has set foot in over thirteen countries. Her books often include elements from her travels. Her three favorite things are dark chocolate, visiting the beach and ocean, and hearing from her readers. Each card, and letter is a treasured gift, like finding a perfect shell upon the beach.

Visit debraparmley.com

BROTHERHOOD PROTECTORS

ORIGINAL SERIES BY ELLE JAMES

Hot SEAL Hawaiian Nights (SEALs in Paradise)

ABOUT ELLE JAMES

ELLE JAMES also writing as MYLA JACKSON is a *New York Times* and *USA Today* Bestselling author of books including cowboys, intrigues and paranormal adventures that keep her readers on the edges of their seats. With over eighty works in a variety of sub-genres and lengths she has published with Harlequin, Samhain, Ellora's Cave, Kensington, Cleis Press, and Avon. When she's not at her computer, she's traveling, snow skiing, boating, or riding her ATV, dreaming up new stories. Learn more about Elle James at www.elle-james.com

Website | Facebook | Twitter | GoodReads | Newsletter | BookBub | Amazon

Follow Elle!
www.ellejames.com
ellejames@ellejames.com

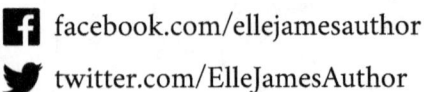
facebook.com/ellejamesauthor

twitter.com/ElleJamesAuthor